Other Books by Lindy Miller

The Magic Ingredient (A Bar Harbor Holiday Novel, Book 1)

Forthcoming From Rosewind Books

Sleigh Bells on Bread Loaf Mountain
Mistletoe Magic (A Bar Harbor Holiday Novel, Book 2)
Regifting Christmas

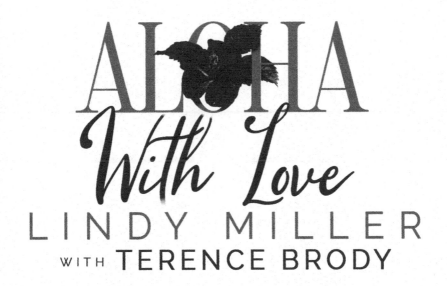

ALOHA
With Love

LINDY MILLER
WITH TERENCE BRODY

Aloha With Love

This is a work of fiction. Names, characters, places, and incidents either are the product of the author's imagination or are used fictitiously. Any resemblance to actual persons, living or dead, or locales is entirely coincidental.

Cover design by Qamber Designs and Media
www.QamberDesignsandMedia.com

ISBN: 978-1-64548-037-2

Published by Rosewind Romance
An imprint of Vesuvian Books
www.RosewindRomance.com

Printed in the United States

10 9 8 7 6 5 4 3 2 1

To my dad

Chapter One

Jenna Burke squared the edge of the architectural model stationed on the conference room table, smoothed her long dark hair behind her ears, and stepped back to examine her work. With dedicated two-story parking garages, a fully stocked fitness center, and a 24-hour coffee bistro, the concept she had designed for Terrace Pines Condominiums was a world unto itself. The luxury residential complex even had its own flagpole out front, the brilliant red and white of the California state flag frozen in a welcoming wave as if beckoning investors—exactly what Jenna hoped today's pitch would bring.

"Perfect."

Almost perfect. Jenna added another patch of shrubbery into a sparse spot of the perimeter foliage. Reevaluating, she replaced the shrubbery with a kou tree, then nodded at her own decision. The dense, leafy canopy and flashy orange blooms of the indigenous Hawaiian tree would offer shade in southern California's balmy summer, and a splash of year-round color. Both would benefit Terrace Pines's landscaping more than just another boring, basic green shrub.

"Just because you're an architect doesn't mean you can't have a little gardener in you, too," Jenna informed the scale model, recounting a cherished morsel of wisdom from her favorite aunt.

Of course, Aunt May was the kind of woman who could sprout a fern in the desert, while Jenna could barely keep the windowsill succulents in her apartment from wilting. Still, the lesson had stuck. Luckily, kou trees were relatively hardy trees, so long as they got a good dose of full sun—something they'd be sure to get in the Golden State.

"Especially when a little bit of a green thumb goes a long way," she finished as she adjusted the kou tree into place.

Jenna made a quick adjustment in her budget, ballparking the impact to the landscaping bid from the last-minute change. By her math, replacing the shrub with the kou tree had an upward effect on the bottom line, but a minimal one and well worth the expense. The colorful tree not only made the bordering foliage more practical *and* more attractive—both to investors and to the complex's eventual residents—but it also offered a long-term advantage in line with Jenna's commitment to sustainable architecture. Aesthetics aside, the slight increase in upfront investment would be well worth the savings over time. Luxury building design was in, but so was green living.

The two didn't have to be mutually exclusive, she thought as she snapped her notebook closed. *Not even in Los Angeles.*

Jenna cleared her throat and spoke aloud to the empty room, testing out the explanation she'd give to justify the minor uptick in her budget. "Kou trees require less trimming than many similarly sized plants and are excellent for roomy landscapes, all without the sprawl of roots that could endanger other plant life or, worse, seep into the surrounding stone edging."

Pause for effect.

"Eventually, such problems would require replacement or repair, both of which would be costly and inconvenient. Not only does a little bit of extra upfront investment ward off those eventual costs, but it actually saves money down the road—*and* brings a little flora of the tropics to Terrace Pines. No other condominium complex in the greater Los Angeles area has a kou tree."

This last was true. It had been too long since Jenna had been back to her island hometown. If there'd been a piece of the island anywhere in the vicinity, she'd have noticed.

Stifling a squeal, Jenna allowed herself a little happy dance. Now all she had to do was sell her idea to Orville Barrington and she'd been one step closer to achieving her biggest dream: breaking ground on one of her own architectural designs. Jenna had yet to meet Barrington, but she knew the type—high profile broker who coordinated deals between wealthy real estate investors, eager commercial realtors, and architectural firms with ambitious junior designers like herself, all anxious to make their mark on the industry. He'd be looking for something new, something fresh. Something with *curb appeal*. Curb appeal was what got high profile investors excited enough to open up their checkbooks.

Luckily, Jenna's concept for Terrace Pines had curb appeal in spades, and the details weren't just in her eye for exterior foliage. Anchored at the edge of Los Angeles's prime waterfront, the luxury condominium complex was the kind of easy upscale living in demand by everyone from active retirees to eager, affluent millennials with young families—or deep pockets. More important, the whole thing just *screamed* sustainable living. Three balcony-edged stories topped with a solar-paneled roof and moored to the coast with large green spaces. A small park with a jogging path encircling the property grounds. Even a water feature in the lobby to bring the fresh outdoors inside, adding to the model's natural mystique without compromising its sleek modern interior.

"I've got your curb appeal right here, Mr. Barrington." Jenna beamed. Satisfied with her final tweaks and finishing touches, she flipped open her laptop and prepared to boot up her presentation for a final run-through. She glanced at the clock over the conference table. Almost showtime.

"Hello, Terrace Pines."

A brusque female voice cut into the room as Jenna made yet another tiny adjustment to her model while her presentation loaded, this time sacrificing a palm for a hibiscus. Her boss, Patti Murray, cup of coffee clutched dependably in her well-manicured grip, leaned against the threshold of the conference room doorway, drinking in her morning brew and Jenna's model in equal measure. Patti was a woman of juxtapositions. Her short, blond, slicked-back hair clearly portrayed her no-nonsense attitude, while her easy smile softened her enough to look approachable, sometimes even friendly. She was one part sweet and two-parts shrewd—precisely what Jenna had hoped for in a mentor when she'd started at Avery Architects.

Jenna took a deep breath, held it for two extra-long beats, and exhaled. "What do you think?"

Patti gave the model an appraising look. She raised a crimson-painted fingernail to her chin, a tactic Jenna had learned signaled deep thought even when one had already arrived at a decision, and narrowed her eyes into a fine line of black mascara.

"It doesn't matter what I think. What matters is what Barrington thinks when he gets here." She winked at Jenna. Then, her mouth twisted into a conspiratorial smirk and her voice dropped to a whisper. "But, for the record, I love it. It's innovative, thoughtful, and attractive. Very Jenna Burke. Well done."

"Thank you." Even though Patti wasn't the one signing her

name on the dotted line, her approval meant almost as much to Jenna as her potential investors' would. Turning her attention back to her presentation, Jenna clicked the slideshow file on her laptop. Her cursor flickered, then turned into spinning pinwheel of death. The screen froze.

Jenna groaned. *Of course.* Of course her machine would choose now to act up. Why wouldn't it?

Ahonui, she thought. Patience.

Patti's voice resumed its usual brisk business tenor. "How are you feeling this morning, Jenna? Are you ready for this?"

"I'm ready." Wait, was she? The words had slipped out of Jenna's mouth before she'd had time to rethink and rearrange them, sort of like her model's landscaping.

Patti nodded and sipped at her coffee. Her lack of response made it easier for Jenna to breathe. If her boss had suspected she wasn't ready to pitch Terrace Pines to Orville Barrington, she would have said so—without hesitation. Instead, Patti pointed at the photograph on Jenna's desktop wallpaper.

"Good. Besides, as long as you have Aunt May looking over your shoulder to make sure the presentation goes perfectly, we have nothing to worry about."

Jenna's focus shifted from the spinning pinwheel to the photo background on her laptop screen. Taken the summer before, she sat cross-legged on the beautiful red sands of a Maui beach, her arms wrapped tight around the shoulders of an older woman wearing white lilies in her silver hair and a bright red muumuu. Jenna was smiling brightly, but Aunt May smiled even brighter— brighter, even, than the blazing sunset crimson of her dress or the blushing blooms of the lei hung about her neck. "We celebrated her seventy-fifth birthday Saturday, but I swear she has the heart of a seventeen-year-old."

Patti blinked. "Please tell me you didn't fly home to Hawaii this weekend?"

"I wish. Had to make do with singing happy birthday over video chat." Jenna dipped her head in the direction of her laptop. "Thank goodness for technology, right? I spent the rest of the weekend getting ready for today."

Her boss clicked her teeth and gave Jenna a thumbs up with the hand not clutching the to-go cup from Jazzy Java. "Good girl. I'm glad you have your priorities straight." Patti took another sip of coffee, then ran her tongue along the sharp edges of her upper teeth, signaling dangerous words ahead. "And what about Darren? Did he have time in his schedule to join you on the birthday video chat?"

Jenna flinched at the mention of her boyfriend, and her insides did a somersault. "We're both so busy with work," she tried, but the explanation felt flat, even to her. She fingered a leafy foliage on her model. Watched the pinwheel spin. Flicked away an invisible piece of dust from her blouse. Letting herself get lost in worries about her flailing relationship would do nothing to help her already-jittery nerves. She could already feel her pulse in her neck as it was. "I hardly see him anymore."

Patti's left eyebrow arched, but she blinked, deftly easing her expression into a diplomatic neutral. "Well, if Barrington's people accept your proposal, you won't have time to see anyone in the next year. So, keep your fingers crossed."

Jenna crossed her fingers and waved them at Patti. "Family, boyfriends, having any kind of social life?" she asked. "Overrated."

Patti's tone was deadpan. "I couldn't agree more."

"I was joking." Jenna knew the put-together workaholic lived alone with her cat, an overweight ginger furball named Meka. She hadn't had a date the entire time Jenna had worked at Avery Architects—nearly five years.

"Really? L-O-L." Patti clicked her tongue. "Did I say that right? Or is it 'loll'? Because I've never actually laughed out loud."

Jenna bit back a laugh. Somehow, this wasn't hard to believe. Patti Murray certainly *had* a sense of humor, but her wit was the kind which had a tendency to sting rather than induce laughter. "Never?"

Patti shrugged and cast a final look at the Terrace Pines model before turning and exiting the conference room. She called back to Jenna over her shoulder, "Never. Good luck."

Chapter Two

J enna was still fretting over ways to ramp up her model's curb appeal and trying to avoid being ensnared by her relationship woes half an hour later when the latter slid into the conference room. Darren Taylor's designer cologne announced his arrival two breaths before Jenna actually saw him. His voice, as smooth as his silk tie, followed shortly thereafter. Both tickled unpleasantly along Jenna's skin, sparking nervous energy into the air.

"Hey, stranger."

"Darren, hi." Jenna forced herself to sound pleasant as her boyfriend bent to give her a quick, perfunctory peck on the cheek. "You're early. The Barrington pitch doesn't start until one."

Of course, if you weren't the realtor on this project, I might never see you at all anymore.

Jenna leaned in for a kiss more substantial than the one Darren had deposited on her face, but he brushed past her, his attention already refocused onto Terrace Pines.

"Wow, this is efficient," he said, his expert realtor gaze surveying the solar panels. Darren's lips moved as he counted the number of exterior windows in relation to the sharp angles of the condominium's exterior and well-placed parking structure. "Not an inch of wasted space. I love it. Barrington should be thrilled."

Jenna sighed. At least they had one thing in common, even if it was only a construction model. Appreciating the same piece of real estate wasn't actually building their relationship, but Jenna supposed at least it was building *something*—right? "You think so?"

"Your concept will certainly bring Terrace Pines into the twenty-first century," Darren said, still eyeing the model. "Beachfront modern. I'm so glad I recommended you for this project."

He recommended *her*? Jenna bit her lip but let the comment slide. Working with Darren was a plus, not a determining factor, even if he had the tendency to think otherwise. "I was able to fit in ten more units than Barrington's client asked for, most of them three-bedroom apartments. The master bedrooms all have an en suite, and two small bedrooms with a jack-and-jill."

"Perfect. The bedrooms can be used as his and hers offices."

"I was going to say children's rooms—" Jenna cleared the catch from her voice, covering it with a cough. "But I guess offices work too."

If Darren had noticed her change in tone, it didn't show. He was still gazing at the model, palms on his knees as he crouched to peer at the greenery Jenna had spent the better part of the morning rearranging. "Sure, for anybody who might be interested in that."

"Like us, right?" The question shot out before Jenna could stop it.

For the first time since he'd entered the conference room, Darren turned his full attention to her. The effort looked almost painful, and the look in his eyes didn't exactly engender confidence. Mostly, he looked bored.

Jenna forced herself not to break eye contact. Instead, she blinked back doubt, doing her best imitation of Patti Murray brand confidence, and tried not to let herself get lost in the sharp curves of Darren's jaw or the deep saltwater green of his eyes as she tried to tweeze intent from his features. When had he started growing a goatee? Jenna had no idea. She was even less sure she liked it. It *did* accentuate the dimple in his chin, the one she used to touch before she kissed him. Not that they'd been anywhere near that level of affection in a long time. When was the last time he'd even hugged her?

"Well, yeah. Maybe someday," he managed eventually. "When we're married. Someday."

Someday. Jenna recognized the tone Darren reserved for his uppity clients, and the playful smiles he thought came across as disarming. The combination smarted twice as much directed at her, curling her lips in the process. Now wasn't the time to dig into the brambles of their relationship, not with Barrington arriving any minute, but considering they'd cancelled every dinner plan for the past three weeks, Jenna had to take the opportunity when she could.

Besides, if Darren wanted to treat her like an uppity client, well, she could be uppity. "Right. You keep saying that. Funny I can't seem to find *someday* on the calendar."

Darren was practiced in the art of shifting conversations away from hazardous topics. "First, let's get the Barrington deal locked, and then we can plan our life together. Landing this deal would go a long way for both of us."

"You realize you're putting our life together in the hands of a billionaire developer saying yes to a PowerPoint and a cheap cardboard model?"

"No, I'm putting our life together in *your* very capable hands." The dimple in Darren's chin expanded as his mouth curved into a smile. He took a step closer, so Jenna had to look up to meet his eyes. "That's why you need to crush this pitch. I went out on a limb to convince Barrington to allow Avery Architects—to allow *you*—to have a bid on this, so don't let me down. This could be a huge beginning for us."

Thanks, Jenna's inner voice snapped. Again, her opportunity was on his merit rather than her own. The thought made her stomach turn. "No pressure," she scoffed.

The dimple in Darren's chin winked under his goatee. "I'm just saying, this would be great for us."

The words were right, but Jenna couldn't help thinking it sounded a lot more like he was saying *me* rather than *us*. "It would be a really nice commission that would go a long way to paying for a wedding," she hinted. When Darren didn't respond, she added, "At the very least, we could officially get engaged. You know, buy a ring. Set a date."

Darren put his arms around her, and Jenna reluctantly allowed herself to be gathered into his embrace. "We both have so much going on right now, and if you get this account, you're going to be the lead architect. Do you really want to be planning a wedding at the same time?"

Did she? Jenna glanced over Darren's shoulder at the photo on her laptop screen. What would Aunt May have said about her planning a wedding and leading her first architectural project at the same time? Jenna didn't have to consider it long. May would have told her to get to work, then cheered her on. "I guess not."

Darren gave a little squeeze. "Of course not. There's no rush. Fiancé is just a title. We can get married anytime."

"It doesn't have to be a big wedding." Jenna muttered, mostly to herself. Frankly, after four years, she'd settle for a ring and vows over takeout pizza if it meant they could finally break ground on their happily-ever-after. She'd even happily pick out her own engagement ring if Darren would just slide it into place on her finger. Heck, even officially moving in together might be enough to satisfy her need for forward momentum. Four years was a long time to be consigned to a single drawer at each other's apartments.

Darren dropped his arms as he moved back to the model, then shifted his attention to Jenna's still-frozen laptop screen. Recognition clicked in his gaze. "How was the virtual birthday party?"

The way he asked didn't give Jenna the impression he was sorry to have missed it. Big surprise. "It was nice. Aunt May asked about you."

"Was your sister there?"

"Sarah was there, with Mike and the kids."

Darren's eyes narrowed almost imperceptibly. "And your dad? Isn't he living with them now?"

Jenna nodded. She already knew what was coming next. It always did.

"How's that working out?" Darren's tone was tight, bordering on sarcastic.

"You know how he is. Dad can be a … handful." It wasn't exactly the right word, but it was the closest thing Jenna could think of with both her boyfriend and Terrace Pines staring her down.

"That's saying it nicely."

Nicely wasn't the right word either, but perhaps Darren was approximating with his choice of vocabulary, too.

Jenna sighed. There wasn't a lot of love lost between her boyfriend and her father. Or most of her family, for that matter. Darren was a big-city guy, and Jenna's family were island people.

It wasn't exactly a perfect match. Sometimes it felt more like they came from different planets than just from across a little bit of ocean. "He likes you. He really does."

Darren gave a wry laugh and ran his fingers through his perfectly gelled dark hair without making a single strand so much as twitch. "He certainly doesn't act like he likes me."

"He'll warm up to you."

"I've known him for four years now. How long does it take for the guy to warm up?"

A pang of irritation flared in Jenna's chest. "It's going to take more than one trip to Maui and a handful of phone calls for him to get to know you."

The two locked eyes for a moment, Jenna's point hitting home.

"You know I don't like to leave the city," Darren said, then waited for Jenna to agree.

She didn't, instead letting the space between them fill with fresh air, quiet streets, lazy afternoons. Relaxation. Quality time.

"How's that huge piece of property doing?" he asked when the silence became too full. "Still sitting around being reclaimed by the tropics?"

Jenna sighed. Of course Darren's thoughts had gone to the one thing he loved above all else—real estate. He was great at his job, but Darren was an opportunist and the large piece of prime Hawaiian property in her family's possession hadn't gone unnoticed. Once Jenna had thought this a good quality—detail-oriented, long-term memory, that sort of thing—but now it was just sort of annoying. "That huge piece of property belongs to my aunt. And her house is right in the middle of it."

"I'm just making an observation," Darren insisted, raising his hands. "It's a substantial piece of land in a place everyone wants to be, and it's just going to waste being left empty like it is since she moved into the retirement community. What do you think she's going to do with it when she … when she goes?"

"*Goes?*" echoed Jenna. "I don't know, and I don't think about it." Now was her turn to change the subject, otherwise she was going to get too flustered to present her pitch. She redirected. "So, tell me more about Orville Barrington."

Darren adjusted his posture and straightened his tie. "Orville Barrington leads a group of investors always looking for projects to put their substantial capital into. He brokers the deal, so the investors remain anonymous, but don't let that fool you. Barrington works on commission, and he knows what he's doing. He's been in business for forty years. My firm has worked with him since the beginning. He's tough."

"And he's here." Darren's eyes darted over Jenna's shoulder to the window behind her, then to his watch. "Men like Barrington like to be early, just to keep everyone on their toes."

Probably why you showed up early today, too. Without looking behind her, Jenna moved to drape a white cloth over the Terrace Pines model. It wouldn't do for Barrington to get a peek before she had the chance to set up the pitch. She let out a sigh of relief when the pinwheel of death on her laptop screen expanded, bringing her PowerPoint presentation with it.

"He's a huge basketball fan, so make a basketball reference," Darren suggested.

"I don't know anything about basketball." Jenna would have appreciated any tips for handling Barrington earlier—say, anytime before he was about to walk through the door. Besides, couldn't any man make a deal without needing a sports reference?

"Just say, 'This deal is a slam dunk!'" Darren said behind her.

"I should go, though. I don't want him to think I'm coaching you in any way.

Coaching. Jenna rolled her eyes. Another sports reference.

"Sort of like what you were just doing?"

"Exactly. Good luck."

"Dinner tonight?" Jenna tried, and hoped the question didn't sound too eager.

Darren was already halfway out the door. "I'm working late, but I'll make it up to you."

Chapter Three

Orville Barrington was a tall black man with salt-and-pepper hair and a neatly trimmed goatee which bore a striking resembles to the one Darren had started to cultivate on his usually clean-shaven chin. He wore an impeccable three-piece suit and a fixed "impress me" expression, both of which told Jenna it was going to take a lot more than a lazy sports metaphor to get him excited about her pitch. She got the impression Orville Barrington didn't get excited about much.

Barrington tapped the toe of his freshly shined shoe against the tile. Apparently, he didn't like to be kept waiting, either.

After a series of handshakes and introductions, Patti, Barrington, Darren, and Jenna filed into the conference room. As soon as everyone was settled around the table, Jenna inhaled a deep gulp of air, held it long enough to help stabilize her breath, and clicked on her laser pointer. Then, she nodded at Patti to begin the presentation queued up on her laptop. When she looked at Darren, he gave her a sly thumbs up from his side of the table.

No pressure. Today was only the biggest pitch of her life—so far. Maybe Darren was right: Terrace Pines could be the starting point for their future together. But, if that were true, what would happen if she failed?

Jenna swallowed the thought.

"Thank you for this opportunity, Mr. Barrington," she began. Her words came out clipped and she smiled, blinked to calm her nerves, and snuck in another sip of air. "According to the National Association of Home Builders, more than half of all condo buyers move out in six years or less. Now, with mortgage rates at an all-time low and single-family developments at an all-time high, how do we make a condo development a can't-miss investment?"

She paused for effect. Barrington blinked. *You're losing him already.*

"The answer," Jenna continued, picking up the pace, "I believe, is community. We construct a complex built for the long-term, both in the sustainability of the structure itself and in its ability to meet the ongoing needs for its residents. We build a place that says home. Community."

Having already positioned the tag line of her pitch, it was time to wow her would-be investor with the model's curb appeal and all the details she'd agonized over for months. Jenna swept the cloth from the model.

"Our concept for Terrace Pines is based on the idea that the complex itself should be more than just a place to call home, but a place to *be* home. It has a jogging path and an indoor/outdoor catering space, coffee bistro, workout space, green spaces, and more. We've maximized all available space, and as a result, have been able to include more units than you asked for. Thirty of those units have two bedrooms, twenty have three bedrooms, and the remainder have one bedroom. People want extra room, even in their beachfront properties."

Jenna closed her mouth before anything about his and hers offices popped out and watched as Barrington eyed her first, then the model. His expression remained stoic as he studied everything from the careful landscaping to the solar panels and other energy-efficient features she'd added. If anything impressed him, it didn't show.

Barrington's gaze swung back to Jenna. "You're very … *sunny* … aren't you?"

"I try to be." Was sunny a bad thing?

He harrumphed and jerked his head back to the model. "You've added in a lot of high-tech hardware. How do you plan on keeping the maintenance fees low?"

"New battery technology combined with solar panels will keep maintenance fees lower than any other condominium complex in the area," Jenna promised. "Thermal cladding for the exterior. Graywater plumbing systems for irrigation for the greenbelts. I estimate we can lower common utility costs by up to seventeen percent."

"Well, I'm not hating it so far."

Resisting the urge to glance at Patti, Jenna forced her face into a confident smile and straightened her posture as Barrington rose from his seat to drift around the table, sizing up the model. He didn't speak for several minutes while he evaluated Terrace Pines from every possible angle. Finally, he took a deep breath and shook his head in a gesture that was a close cousin to approval.

"Nice looking," he decided. "A little—" His eyes slid back at Jenna. "Sunny. But it's not terrible."

Not terrible? The comment stung, but it wasn't a pass. A good sign, right?

"It's more than looks," Patti cut in, her voice brisk and professional. Realtors like Darren and his firm might bring in heavy hitters, but Patti Murray knew how to wheel and deal. She could sell a concrete box to a hotel tycoon on a bad day. "This build has personality. Longevity."

Nodding, Barrington returned to his chair and Jenna and Patti took their seats across from him. They waited patiently as he reviewed the printed materials prepared for him. When he was finished scanning the pages, Barrington stacked them and crossed his hands atop the papers. "I've heard your marketing pitch, now let's get down to brass tacks. How many units do you have, exactly?"

Jenna's answer was automatic. "Sixty-six. Ten more than you asked for."

"And the parking garage is—"

"In the sub levels," she finished. "So there is no wasted real estate."

"No pool?" Barrington raised an eyebrow in Jenna's direction.

"And give back the ten units?"

"I like the way you think," Barrington pressed, "but a condo complex without a pool? A pool is a strong selling point."

Jenna had anticipated this question and had an answer at the ready. "There's a public pool nearby, and the property Darren has identified as a suitable location is within walking distance to the beach. We can work a deal with the town to offer a discount to your tenants, so you get the best of all worlds—a members-only pool your investors don't have to maintain or sacrifice space for, fast access to the beach for tenants, and the income from ten additional units."

Barrington reclined in his chair and looked impressed. He took off his glasses and picked up the papers, reading them this time rather than skimming. The left corner of his mouth twitched—not exactly enough to be considered a smile, but something close to approval anyway. "Sunny and smart, interesting combination. Tell me about the catering space."

"The units are spacious for a single person, a couple, or even a small family to host a decent size gathering. But if a tenant wants to throw, say, an engagement party with fifty guests, they can rent the catering space for half of what they'd pay to rent a catering hall. And when a tenant isn't renting the space, you can rent it out to the public—utilize it as a separate revenue stream."

"How much do you think we can rent it for?"

Jenna smiled, happy to have captured Barrington's full attention as she slid a sheet of paper with additional numbers across the table. "I ran an analysis based on what mid to top-tier restaurants charge in the neighborhood to accommodate fifty to seventy-five people."

Barrington's lip twitched even higher when he saw the number. "Not bad." He set the papers down, gave the model another scrutinizing glance. "Not great. I'm not sure the coffee shop is necessary."

"I am," Patti chimed in. She lifted her coffee cup in salute. "There's over eight hundred coffee shops in the LA area, but none of them are unique to Terrace Pines. People will pay for the privilege of an on-site café just for them. Sometimes it's not just about the availability of something, but the exclusiveness of it."

The man's eyes narrowed, but he nodded. Patti made a fair point.

"And unlike area restaurants," Jenna continued, "our bistro model includes two large glass doors that open out to the garden, giving guests the additional option to enjoy outdoor seating as well."

"A garden? How many additional units could you have included if you hadn't given up valuable space?"

Barrington's sharp tone cut Jenna to the quick. "We could add in more units, but that wouldn't be as aesthetically pleasing, or the best use of space in my opinion."

He held up his palm in the universal gesture for pause. "Well, Miss Burke, *aesthetically* my investors will care more about the ROI on any additional units than they will on a bunch of plants. Pretty flowers and greenspaces are what landscaping is for."

"Yes, but—"

"What's the total cost on the build?"

Jenna cleared her throat. "Construction cost is five percent under your target budget—"

"*Five* percent?"

"That's correct."

"I presume the low margin is due to your—" He flicked the kou tree, knocking it aside. "Finishing touches?"

Jenna's heart flipped. So much for curb appeal. Sure, her pitch could have included substantially deeper savings, but she'd tried to recoup for upfront investment in long-term gains. "Our concept may be a bit more costly upfront, but we are confident the additional elements we've included will make the property more attractive to investors, and will appeal to residents looking for a long-term housing solution. And, with the green roof and solar panels, combined with new battery technology that can store solar energy, Terrace Pines will save tens of thousands over the coming years. A smaller margin upfront will equate to substantially higher returns down the road."

Remembering Darren's coaching, Jenna pointed to one more feature right in front of the building. "Oh, and we have a flagpole. It's a grand slam!"

Barrington shuffled his papers into a neat stack and pushed himself up from the table. "I'm a basketball fan."

❧

Patti stuck her head into Jenna's office just as she finished packing up for the day. She'd moved the Terrace Pines model into her office, where it still sat uncovered atop her desk. Jenna had rearranged the foliage half a dozen more times since Barrington left, shepherded out by Darren, who hadn't bothered to say goodbye. The kou tree Barrington had knocked over still lay unrooted.

"Grand slam?" Patti asked, sipping her afternoon coffee. "Where'd you come up with that one?"

Jenna's shoulders sagged. She decided against telling Patti it had been Darren's last-minute tip. "I got my sports terms mixed up."

"You did great, Jenna," Patti offered by way of comfort. "You're very talented and the work you put into this deal really showed today, sports terms notwithstanding."

Did she? "I took some chances with the green roof and solar panels." *And the landscaping.*

Patti shrugged down another sip of coffee. "Like you said in the pitch, a few extra upfront dollars will save them money down the road. You want long-term, you have to think long-term."

"But it will cost upfront. Barrington balked at only five percent." Jenna gazed at her model, thumbed at the downed kou tree. Long-term thinking might have short-term consequences.

"Listen to me, Jenna," said Patti. "Creativity is all too often stymied by the almighty dollar, but that's why this business needs people like you who push boundaries and think outside the box. You created a beautiful complex with an incredible amount of personality for its residents—and it makes good business sense."

Jenna digested Patti's words and tried to remember she'd been in this business a lot longer than Jenna had. "So, what do you think? Do we have a shot?"

"Barrington may have rushed out of here, but he took the papers with him. That's a good sign. We'll just have to wait and see. Try not to obsess over it—it'll give you wrinkles." She eyed Jenna over the brim of her coffee cup and redirected. "Darren rushed out of here quick on Barrington's heels. Isn't tonight date night?"

"He's working late." Jenna's lips curled at the bitter taste of the words. It *would* have been nice to spend the evening with her boyfriend, whether they talked about the deal or not. Or would it? Knowing Darren, the deal would probably be *all* he wanted to talk about, and Jenna needed a break from the topic before she drove herself crazy. It wasn't like he was going to be interested in talking about anything more material to their relationship, like their *actual* relationship.

"On date night?" Patti pressed.

Jenna shrugged. "He's very ambitious?" She didn't love the way her explanation ended in a question. It was decidedly *un-*sunny, and although Barrington had made it sound like a criticism, Jenna rather liked being sunny. In her experience, sunny places were the warmest ones.

Patti's eyebrow rose toward the ceiling. "Then you two are perfect for each other."

"I suppose."

As much as Jenna appreciated having a boss so supportive and accommodating on work-life balance, she didn't feel comfortable sharing more about how she and Darren weren't exactly working toward the same end goal. Come to think of it, she wasn't even sure she was comfortable admitting the truth to herself. *That's probably not a good sign*, she thought.

Fortunately, Patti's sensible intuition extended beyond her architectural savvy. She paused for a moment and, stepping farther into Jenna's office, extended the closest thing to motherly advice Jenna thought the hard-nosed businesswoman capable of.

"Sleep in tomorrow, boss's orders. Take some time in the morning to enjoy an extra cup of coffee. If anything comes up here, I'll call you."

Jenna managed a weak smile. "Thanks."

Patti waved Jenna's words away and shot a look over her shoulder as she strode out the office door. "This isn't about boys, it's about performance. You hit it out of the park today—" Patti paused to let them both enjoy her own sports reference. "You've earned it."

Alone again in her office, Jenna stared at her model of Terrace Pines and reflected on her day, trying to see it from Patti's point of view. All things considered, the meeting with Barrington had gone better than anticipated—not perfect, sure, but not terrible, either. He'd been pleased with the extra units and the catering plan, but less than enthusiastic about the estimated construction costs coming only five percent below target. Patti was right—creativity was often stymied by the dollar because no matter how much investors talked about wanting something new and innovative, when it came down to brass tacks, money still mattered most. Real estate investors wanted buildings that would last, but they didn't generally relish the idea of waiting longer than necessary to make a return. What a funny and frustrating dance—build for the long haul, invest for the short. Things like sustainable building and green living sounded great on marketing materials, but often lost their luster on the balance sheet.

Had she done enough? Jenna's career might depend on this project—and on Darren Taylor and Orville Barrington, two unknown variables. Right now, she could only hope she'd wowed them all with her design and research. Otherwise, she didn't know if she had enough curb appeal to bolster her future in architectural design, much less pull off a passion project like Terrace Pines.

Well, she'd done her best. All she could do now was wait and see. *And*, Jenna considered, gazing at the framed photo of her and Darren on her desk, *at least you don't have a wedding to plan.*

Chapter Four

By the time she arrived in her office two hours later than usual the next morning, Jenna had managed to work her way through just about every emotion she had. It had a been a long night, but she had pulled many all-nighters in her brief career already. Losing another few hours of sleep worrying herself half to death over the state of Terrace Pines was nothing out of the ordinary.

Despite her fruitless attempts to see things Patti's way, Jenna had left her office the day before weary and deflated, wallowing in worst-case-scenario blues until around dinnertime, after which she'd gotten a second wind and started reflecting on the day more positively. A late yoga session and warm bubble bath later, Jenna had climbed into bed, already working her way back up from rock bottom. She *had* done pretty well, all things considered, and she'd poured her heart into the Terrace Pines concept. Barrington's wealthy backers might be rich, but they would be downright silly if they turned down her pitch.

Her model had been spot-on and her delivery flawless, even if she had mixed up her silly sports terms. At the end, it was simple: there wasn't another architect in town who could offer the same level of style and function of her design—not at five percent below target and not with the details she'd put so much care into.

And, she'd decided, being *sunny* was definitely a good thing. And a community garden beat out ten additional units any day. Darren hadn't called, and Jenna hadn't texted. He was going to have a lot of work to do if he was going to make up for missing their date night and blowing her off after the biggest pitch of her career so far.

A bouquet of flowers isn't going to cut it this time, Jenna thought as she breezed past her office and the vase full of apology roses already waiting on her desk. Just to put a little extra pep in her step, she'd even worn her favorite heels to work this morning—bright bubblegum pink pumps that gave her an extra half-inch of height and clicked when she walked on the office's ceramic tile floors. *Sunny.*

In the small break room, Jenna poured two cups of coffee, added a splash of milk to one, and clicked her way to Patti's office. "Any news?"

The needle-sharp expression on Patti's face popped Jenna's bubble. "Barrington called. They're going with a proposal from Ken Johnson Architects."

Black liquid slipped over the edge of the coffee mugs, scalding Jenna's hands. It could have been her nerves or the lack of sleep catching up with her, but spilled coffee was spilled coffee—*hot.* After safely setting down the mugs, Jenna mopped up the mess with a tissue from the box on Patti's desk and collapsed into one of the two guest chairs in the room. "But we gave them everything he wanted and more, and still came in under budget."

Patti shrugged and lifted the cup of coffee sans milk. She always said she liked her coffee black, just like she liked the numbers in her bank account. "Johnson's firm convinced him they can come in ten percent under budget. Ten is more than five."

"Money," grumbled Jenna. She'd known it. She could offer Barrington's investors every bell and whistle, give them every buzzword in today's real estate marketing vocabulary, but in the end it all boiled down to who could offer the best build with the biggest discount.

"Almighty dollar," Patti corrected. "Creativity stymie, pitch breaker."

Jenna still couldn't wrap her head around it. "So, that's it? They can do it cheaper, so they get the account?"

"That's what he said."

Visions of the Terrace Pines model still on her desk haunted Jenna's thoughts. "I really thought I checked all Barrington's boxes, Patti."

"Sometimes the boxes we don't see are the ones that need to be checked the most."

Jenna reached for her own mug and chugged down a larger-than-ladylike gulp, trying not to feel like a failure. "What amenities do they offer? Do they have a rentable party space to create revenue? Is their concept energy efficient, like ours? Will the extra five percent investors save now offset the tens of thousands of dollars of savings our design promises down the road?" Her voice rose, grew nasal. "Did they replace their useless shrubbery with kou trees and hibiscus?"

Patti leaned across the desk, elbows on the table, and set her chin on top of her hands. She gave Jenna a moment to catch her breath, and then spoke slowly, her tone firm but kind. "I don't know anything about their model, and it really doesn't matter. Barrington's investors are simply too shortsighted to see past upfront costs."

Jenna squirmed, and Patti continued, rising and walking

toward the other side of her office. She stood framed by the dozens of certificates of accomplishments lined on the wall behind her. This posture wasn't accidental; Patti was positioning herself right where she needed to be to deliver an important business lesson supported by her wall of credibility.

"Jenna, you did a fantastic job with the Terrace Pines model. This is just how it is. You can do everything right and still not win the bid. There'll be other opportunities. Sometimes losing a job is the best possible outcome. Let it go. Besides, just because Barrington's people rejected the concept, what you built for Terrace Pines still has legs. The right investors will come along."

Her milked-down coffee tasted sour on her tongue, and it was all Jenna could do not to sigh as she pushed herself up from the chair. Finding another investor interested in the Terrace Pines project was not impossible, but it was also not guaranteed. No wonder Darren hadn't called. "I was so confident."

Back at her desk, Jenna slumped in her chair and glared at the model of Terrace Pines. Patti was right, of course. If getting the most bang for their buck was Barrington's investors prime directive, she could have whittled costs down to the bones, been dissatisfied with her own work, and still have lost the deal. But surely there was something else she could have done to earn their buy-in while still delivering her dream concept? Maybe she should have cut the garden and put in a few more units? Or added more single bedroom units, rather than two and three-bedrooms? Cut out the tropical flora and left in the boring old shrubs?

Perhaps it had been naïve to think she could design a luxury condominium community attractive enough to appeal to long-term residents. If the National Association of Home Builders said condo residents stayed six years or less, who was she to challenge them? Jenna hadn't even lived in her current apartment for three.

Of course, she'd assumed she and Darren would have moved in together by year four of their relationship, but that didn't appear to be happening anytime soon—not unless she wanted to embrace the idea of his and hers office spaces.

Not likely.

Jenna's laptop chimed, signaling an incoming video call and pushing her out of her meditative funk. A photo of the caller flashed on her screen—silver hair and crimson dress—and Jenna's worries instantly dissipated.

"Aunt May."

She clicked the button to accept, and Aunt May's face filled the screen. Behind her, palm trees and ocean waves dazzled in the sunny Hawaiian landscape from her wicker rocking chair on the porch of her retirement community. May looked a little more tired than she had at her online birthday bash the past weekend, and perhaps a hair older, but still every bit as exuberant.

"*Aloha*, Peanut. How did the pitch go?"

Jenna sighed. Sharing the bad news with her aunt was three times worse than experiencing it herself, even if May was the only one who could have possibly made her feel better. "I crashed and burned. The client passed for a cheaper pitch."

The old woman smiled, and the wrinkles around her eyes cracked so her eyes sparkled in the late afternoon sun. "You don't look burned to me. You look beautiful."

"Thank you, Aunt May."

"I know how hard you worked on this. I know how much it means to you."

"I spent so much time on it. Really thought I'd nailed it…" Jenna dropped her face into her hands. "I even missed your special birthday. And for what? It was all over in five minutes. I should have flown down to be with you."

Aunt May waved away her apologies from the other side of the screen. "Chin up, young lady. Did *you* love how your design turned out?"

Jenna stared at the model on her desk. Was it failure that made it look so much less appealing now than it had just twenty-four hours before, or was her design just terrible? "I thought I did, but now I don't know what to think."

"You keep doing what you love, and success will follow. I promise. *A'a i ka hula, waiho i ka maka'u i ka hale.*"

Put on your dancing shoes and leave shame at home. The Hawaiian proverb encouraged one to take pride in themselves, regardless of what others thought. It was Aunt May's way of reminding her not to see the value of her work through anyone's eyes but her own.

It sounded so easy when her aunt said it, though Jenna wasn't so sure. "But—"

"No *buts* allowed," Aunt May cut in. "All *buts* do is keep you down in the dumps. *Yes, ands* are what keep you going."

Jenna felt her mouth curve into a smile in spite of her pessimistic mood. "Some island wisdom from the Queen of Maui?"

The old woman nodded, laughing. "*E hele me ka pu'olo.*"

"What's that one? My Hawaiian's rusty."

Aunt May snickered. "Come home more often and it wouldn't be," she teased. "We miss you, Peanut. Me, your dad, even your sister. You need a good dose of the best medicine the island has to offer—sunshine, saltwater, and enough room to breathe some fresh life into your lungs."

Jenna's smile deepened, turned genuine. "I'll come for a visit—and soon, I promise. I love you."

On screen, Aunt May brandished a mischievous grin. She winked and leaned in closer to the screen. "I got a bunch of oldsters waiting for me to play bingo, and I love taking their bingo bucks from them. *Aloha wau iā 'oe*, Peanut."

With a goodbye wave, Jenna pressed the button to end the call just as her phone buzzed, signaling an incoming text message.

Lunch? It was from Darren.

She thought about ignoring it but changed her mind. *Sure.*

Chapter Five

The decision to break away for lunch with Darren had been difficult, but so was the prospect of sitting in her office, staring at her failed concept for Terrace Pines. If Jenna was going to choose between the two methods of torture, at least she could opt for the one outside. Aunt May hadn't been wrong about the rejuvenating qualities of the outdoors. What was the saying—fresh air clears the mind and refreshes the soul?

Summers in LA ran hotter than they did in Hawaii. Darren was already waiting at a two-person outside table at the busy hillside eatery when Jenna slid into the chair across from him, fanning herself cool.

The new goatee might suit his face after all, she decided. It tickled her skin when Darren leaned across the table and pecked her cheek. "I'm glad we're getting lunch. I need someone to talk to today."

Darren's face shifted. "You didn't get the job."

His deadpan delivery told Jenna it hadn't been a guess. "I take it you heard the news."

"Barrington's going with another architect. Ken Johnson's firm was able to offer a better bottom line. I'm sorry, Jenna."

Well, great news travels fast. Of course, if Patti already knew about Barrington's decision, naturally Darren would, too. A dark cloud descended over the sunny afternoon as Jenna considered Darren's position in the deal. Hopefully her loss hadn't cost him his commission, too. "Are *you* going to be okay?"

Across the table, Darren stiffened. "I guess I'll have to be. He's also decided to go with another realtor."

There was something else written between the lines of Darren's statement, something he didn't say but she heard just the same: *and it's your fault.* He had been the one who had recommended her, after all.

Jenna tore at a piece of the complimentary bread the waitress had dropped off. Carbs were the gateway drug to self-loathing and bloat, but right now she needed a little bit of comfort food in her life. "Lunch together will cheer us up," she tried, hunting for the silver lining. "It's been a long time since we've been able to fit a spontaneous lunch into our busy daytime schedules."

There, something she didn't say either—lunch was a perfect time to meet with anxious real estate clients. Darren probably needed those, considering her blunder had cost him Barrington. She'd expected him to agree, but instead Darren sat back in his chair, his body language hard.

"Right?" Jenna pushed the basket of bread away, already feeling its weight in the pit of her stomach.

"I didn't think about the timing."

"Timing of what?"

Darren sighed and the sound came out rough, like he'd been thinking about something thick and unpleasant. He ran a hand through his hair and this time he did it rough enough to upset his carefully combed locks. "Here's the thing…"

Jenna's heart flipped in her chest. She could feel the bread rising back up from her stomach. "What thing?"

"I'm getting to it."

"To what?"

Darren sighed again, crossed his arms. "You're not making this any easier."

"What?" Jenna asked, but she had a bad feeling she already knew. In her experience, it was never a good sign when a guy started being vague about important topics. Talking in circles around the subject before getting to the point was distancing behavior, the kind of tactic people used when they'd already disconnected themselves emotionally from the subject at hand and just needed to get the words out to finish the deal. "What 'this' am I not making any easier?"

"You see, I've been thinking..."

Jenna raised an eyebrow. "About?"

Darren cleared his throat, waiting as the waitress delivered their orders before continuing. Jenna had ordered her usual salad and avocado toast, though she was really more in the mood for a sandwich. Darren had opted for the daily special. Cake sounded better than either. Jenna made a mental note to pop by a bakery on her way back to the office.

"About us. We're both very much dedicated to our careers—"

"And to each other," Jenna inserted hopefully, but Darren's reaction told her it was the wrong move. Nothing said *foot in mouth* like a wince.

Darren spread his hands out in front of him as if hunting for the right words. His tongue flicked out, ran along the edge of his teeth.

Dangerous words ahead. Reality slammed into Jenna. The daytime meeting. His distancing behavior. The freaking light lunch in a public setting. "You're breaking up with me."

"I just feel like I need more time to focus on my career." Daren pivoted away from a direct answer. "We both do. Surely, a career-oriented woman like yourself can understand that."

Jigsaw pieces assembled in Jenna's thoughts, and she didn't like the picture they showed. Sure, they'd been going through a bit of a rough patch lately, and they'd both been so fixated on the Terrace Pines pitch. But breaking up? This was not the outcome she'd anticipated. "Wait, you're breaking up with me because we lost the Barrington deal?"

"I just think we need to slow things down. Take our time."

Jenna licked her lips, tasted salt, and snapped. "You mean because dating for *four years* is rushing things?"

Darren rolled his eyes, sat back in his chair. "We just don't have the right foundation laid. Terrace Pines would have been a year's worth of living for both of us. We would've been able to put a lot of equity into our relationship bank."

Seriously? Jenna could understand how Darren's preoccupation with his rising trajectory in real estate might be more important than his relationship with her. She could also understand, however, that he'd held on just long enough not to land the large commission Terrace Pines would have brought in. If she'd landed the Barrington deal, would Darren have still cut her loose? If she'd hit that ten percent mark, would they be setting a date right now instead of breaking up over lunch?

Did it matter?

"I've never really thought of our relationship as a checking account. I always thought love should be surrounded by little heart emojis, not dollar signs."

"Well, maybe dollar signs are a better measure," Darren shot back. "This is the rest of our lives we're talking about—not exactly something we should be winging as we go along."

"How romantic." Jenna picked at another piece of bread. Nothing said true love like finances. Had they always been so far apart on how they measured their relationship? She was also fairly certain she'd never *winged* anything, other than her eyeliner.

"Now you're being flighty."

Jenna stood from the table and slung her bag over her shoulder. "No, now I'm being done, Darren."

"That's not what I'm asking for." The words were right, but the way they sounded coming off Darren's lips wasn't. Mostly it sounded like he didn't really care—he'd just prefer she didn't make a scene. "Not an end, a pause."

"Either way is a stop, Darren, and putting a relationship that's going nowhere on hold just doesn't make sense to me. What are we waiting for? I hope you get the life of your dreams. I really do. But I see now, it's not with me. I need heart emojis, Darren. The dollar signs aren't anywhere near as important. Not to me."

With that, Jenna excused herself from the table, taking the last bit of complimentary bread—and her dignity—along with her.

꘎

Jenna had been staring at the model of Terrace Pines, but she'd long since stopped seeing it. She'd turned over the framed photo of her and Darren on her desk, too, so she didn't have to look at it either. Things had started off so promising this morning. A little uneasy, sure, but she'd still had hope about her pitch and a boyfriend. Now it was mid-afternoon, and she'd managed to lose both her potential client and her future husband.

"Way to go, Jenna," she mocked herself with a dry laugh.

"Really bang up job. Way to go."

A soft knock on the door turned her attention. It was Patti, coffee in hand as always.

Whatever the woman had intended to say died unspoken on her lips. "You're not still upset about Barrington? Seriously, let it go."

Jenna shook her head, not ready to bump Orville Barrington back to the top of her list of things to beat herself up over just yet. "I just blew up my life over avocado toast."

Patti grimaced. "What's avocado toast?" She blinked. "I mean, I'm so sorry. Why?"

"Darren invited me to lunch. I wasn't going to go, but Aunt May cheered me up and it's been *weeks* since he and I spent any time together that wasn't work related. On the drive over, I thought everything was going to be okay." The threat of tears stung behind Jenna's eyes, but she blinked them back. Her voice trembled. "Instead, he told me I'm distracting him from his career—and that we're not adding enough equity into our *relationship account.*"

"Relationship account?" Patti grimaced. "Oh boy. Even I wouldn't use that line." She grabbed a tissue from a nearby box, took a second, appraising look at Jenna, then thrust the whole box over.

Jenna covered her face with her hands and mumbled into her palms. Her breath came out of her in waves, pulling up from her toes. "I know. I was the one who officially called it quits, but I still feel like he left me a long time ago."

Patti's hand landed on Jenna's shoulder. "I'm not really the hugging type, but we'll get you through this. Just ... take some deep breaths."

Jenna nodded and took a gulp of air. Tears had muddied her contacts and her vision was blurry, but even so, she could see Patti staring down at her, her expression a mix between professional frustration and friendly empathy.

"Take the rest of the day off," Patti instructed. "Call it a day."

No mascara appeared on Jenna's fingertips when she wiped at her eyes. A small victory. "I have work to do. I can't come in late *and* leave early."

Patti rolled her eyes. "Yes, you can. We all have those days. Go home and focus on you. Darren is just one tiny fish in a sea full of—"

"No more metaphors, please," Jenna groaned. Sports she'd never liked, but she was still a fan of seafood.

Patti started. "I'm sorry, you're right. Let's call a spade a spade. Darren Taylor is a jerk, plain and simple. I never liked him for you." She turned from the office but stopped in the doorway. "Look, Jenna, I know I don't seem like the pajama-wearing, gallon-of-ice-cream-eating, rom-com-watching type of girl, but when a man breaks my heart … I break out the Häagen Dazs. It's absolutely essential in recovering from a breakup. So go home, stop at the store and pick up something bad for your waistline, and if you need me, please let me know—and take the afternoon *off*. I don't want to see so much as a single email."

On her desk, Jenna's cell phone rang, and Patti used the opportunity to evacuate herself from Jenna's office. Jenna groaned when she saw her sister's name on the screen.

She thumbed the button to pick up the call and forced a smile into her voice. "Hi, Sarah. How are you?"

Her sister's voice on the other end of the line came across muffled. It sounded like she'd been crying. "Jenna, how fast can you get here?"

A feeling of impending disaster crashed into Jenna for the second time that day. She braced for the worst. "Why? What's happened?" The muffled quality in Sarah's voice was tears. "It's Aunt May. Her heart ... it finally gave out." Sarah made a hiccupping sound, sniffling twice before responding. When she spoke again, her voice cracked. "She's gone, Jen."

The world stopped around Jenna as an image of her aunt, ready to take her fellow retirement home friends for all they had in midday bingo, flashed through her mind. "No! That can't be possible. I just talked to her this morning!"

More sniffles from the other side of the line. "Can you come home?" There was a pause, heavy with the worry. "Please?"

Jenna was already gathering her purse, Darren and Terrace Pines all but forgotten. "I'll be there tomorrow. I'm on my way."

Despite Patti's insistence she not do any more work for the rest of the day, Jenna clicked open her inbox, ready to fire off a quick email she'd need to take a little longer than the afternoon off, but the swirling pinwheel of death flashed onto the screen, freezing her in place. There was no time to waste on an email. Jenna shut her laptop, shoved the machine in her backpack, and headed to Patti's office.

Chapter Six

Jenna resisted the urge to tap her heels impatiently as Patti wrapped up a call with client.

It was only a few minutes of waiting, but things had a way of stretching on forever when a person was busy trying to keep their heart from spilling out through their eyes. Jenna was doing this now, doing her best to focus on Patti's uplifted index finger—the one which promised she'd be just a minute longer and to hang on tight—and keep the tears from rising past the waterline.

Jenna Burke, you will not cry at work, she scolded herself. Not over boyfriends, bad pitches, or even upon hearing news she'd known was coming but had not at all been prepared to hear. It was one of her top rules as a professional businesswoman. Emotions were for anyplace other than the office. They had all known Aunt May's days were short, but such knowledge provided little comfort now—not that it ever would. What would Jenna do without her?

"This is not the first time we've planned a library," Patti was saying into the receiver, her tone as knowledgeable and reassuring as it was definitive. "I can show you what we've done in the past and we can incorporate what you like into your plan."

Patti's uplifted finger swam in Jenna's watery vision and she adjusted her stance in the doorway, forcing her expression to remain smooth and her body—which wanted very badly to tremble—to stay still.

Be a statue. Jenna did her best to listen to her own instructions. It wasn't easy; even in the best of times, Jenna had never been very good at standing still. She needed to move, to create. It was part of why she'd become an architect—so she could channel all that energy into building something from nothing. It hadn't taken her very far yet, but she was still a long way from giving up hope it eventually would.

"And we'll figure out a way to keep the nostalgia of the old town while bringing modern amenities worthy of a state-of-the-art library. This building is the centerpiece of your town, and it should be grand but welcoming," Patti said dramatically. She stopped and listened for a beat as she waited for the client on the other end of the line to come around to her way of thinking.

The speech was so convincing that Jenna momentarily was able to look beyond her troubles and remember how much she admired Patti Murray. If, in a few years, she was half the architect—and the businesswoman—Patti was, then all of the bumps along the way would be worth it.

If.

A beat of silence passed while Jenna forced her thoughts to wander to anything other than Orville Barrington, Darren Taylor, and now Aunt May. In the space of just a few hours—the blink of an eye, really—she'd lost them all.

Patti smiled as she resumed control of the conversation. "I'm glad you agree. I look forward to meeting with you."

Another beat.

"Okay, great." Patti nodded and leaned in the direction of the phone's cradle, ready to drop the receiver in as the matter had apparently been sorted. "We'll talk to you soon." She shifted her attention to Jenna. "What's up, Jenna?"

Jenna opened her mouth to speak, but everything she'd been working to hold back rushed out and she sagged against the doorframe, bawling. Hands over her face, tears pouring out of her eyes, mixing with the wetness on her cheeks until the whole mess soaked through her fingers and left wet blots on the sleeve of her blouse. Her mascara was ruined, that much was sure. She could only hope her reputation as a professional businesswoman would remain intact. Surely one crying episode wouldn't damage that? Not when it was over something so serious.

Jenna hoped not.

It took longer than she liked to stop the flow of tears, and through her fingers, Jenna saw Patti jump out of her chair. She grabbed a tissue from the box on her desk, then tossed it to the side, pulled Jenna inside the office, and shut the door behind them. If one was to cry in public, best to do it behind the safety of a closed door— even if Patti's executive office was a window-walled fishbowl.

"Oh my goodness, girl." Patti managed to sound sympathetic and not pitying. "I told you there'll be other accounts. Jenna, you really need to pull yourself together."

Jenna sucked in a ragged sob. "It's not that."

Patti's brows knit together. "The Darren thing? Honey, he's not worth it. I know he's handsome and successful and he kills it at parties—"

"Are you trying to make me feel *worse?*" Jenna wailed, having forgotten entirely about Darren's good qualities. Now that Patti mentioned them, maybe she should allocate one or two sobs for her ex, not that he deserved them.

"He's also selfish, self-absorbed, and a total jerk," Patti finished as she fed Jenna another tissue from the box. "He doesn't deserve you!"

"It's not him either," managed Jenna, finally able to speak without the interruption of sobs and hiccups. Her tears were stopping, but an empty achiness was setting in their place, the kind that burrowed deeper than botching a pitch or being dumped. It felt like someone had carved a hole inside of her, sucking out every scrap of the optimistic outlook she'd started the day with. "It's my Aunt May. She's ... gone."

Patti blinked a few times, her expression playing catch-up with her thoughts. "I thought her health had been on the uptake. You didn't mention ... You just celebrated her birthday?"

"She was going better for a while, but her heart..." Jenna shrugged. May *had* looked tired this morning on their video chat. Tired and old. Why hadn't Jenna noticed something was wrong? She knew why—she'd been too busy wallowing in her own self-pity.

"Oh, honey, I'm so very sorry for your loss."

Jenna sighed. "Thank you. I think she was ready." A fresh well of tears rose into her eyes, blurring her vision again. "But I'll miss her."

Patti laid a cool palm against Jenna's shoulder. The gesture felt unpracticed but was still appreciated. Jenna used a tissue to wipe at her runny mascara and sniffed her way back into control of her emotions.

"I feel like she was preparing us all for it—at her birthday, I mean. Don't they always say you know when the time is coming? I guess Aunt May knew. That's why she had the whole family get together, even if we could only be online."

Jenna smiled, reflecting. Beside her, Patti relaxed a fraction as she sensed Jenna calming down.

"Aunt May was like a second mother to me ... but one who didn't give me a curfew or make me do my homework," Jenna said, laughing a little at the memory. "She did all the things good aunts are supposed to do, like let me eat sugary cereal like Golden Puffs and Choco Krispers."

"I loved Choco Krispers!" Patti exclaimed, finally finding a thread of conversation she could latch onto. "They turned regular milk into chocolate milk. So delicious."

"I know, right?" Jenna's sobs had turned to giggles. Emotions were funny like that—they didn't always come out as expected, and rarely ever linearly. Losing Aunt May hurt, but she'd given Jenna so many wonderful memories it was hard to stay sad in the presence of all those beautiful moments. "And when my mom died—I was only sixteen—my sister had gone off to college and it was hard, but Aunt May was there for me. Always. She stepped right in and helped me get through those teen years. Helped my *dad* get through them, and he definitely needed her as much as I did. Being a teenager was hard."

Patti gave Jenna's shoulder a little squeeze as she pulled away, taking what remained of her tissue box with her to her position behind the relative safety of her desk. "Teenage years are awful years," she commiserated. "I don't think anybody comes through them unscathed. Myself, I've erased all memory of high school."

Jenna bit back a laugh. She'd never considered Patti as anything other than what she was today. It was hard to imagine the savvy leader of Avery Architects as an awkward girl with a bad haircut, doodling her name in hearts on her school notebooks.

Balling the black-smeared tissue in her fist, Jenna took a deep breath, collected her thoughts, and, eyeing her favorite bubblegum pink heels, pushed herself to her feet. Her outburst had been unfortunate, but it had had the added benefit of clearing her head. Confronted with the loss of her aunt, everything else seemed trivial.

"I need to go home to Maui."

"I totally understand."

"I'm sorry for crying," Jenna added.

Patti shook her head, widening her eyes with relief. "Just don't let it happen again," she joked. "I'm kidding. Sort of. Is there anything I can do?"

"No, but thank you." How long would it take for the hole dug inside her to fill? "A little time with my family is all I need."

"Take as much as you need," Patti said, then added, "Just check your email when you can."

Chapter Seven

Sarah Maxwell, Jenna's older sister, lived in the suburban part of the island, in a two-story Cape Cod.

The house was two tiers of creamy white edged in butter-yellow trim and surrounded by the kind of flowerbeds that people either had to stay home to maintain or employ meticulous landscaping services to service. During the holidays, Sarah's husband Mike strung thousands of twinkling mini lights from the house's eaves and over its box hedges; in spring, everything sprang to life in colorful shades of pink and red. The overall effect was a sweet, quaint home—the kind found on the covers of home decorating magazines. The colorful, birthday cake house was especially fitting for Sarah, who, besides sharing Jenna's love of landscaping, was the only real baker in the family.

Jenna's taxi had just pulled in the driveway when the front door of her sister's house opened. Sarah came rushing out as Jenna retrieved her luggage from the trunk and made her way to the front porch. An old man in an even older car idled down the street. He smiled and waved at Jenna as he passed, and she returned a half-hearted gesture. When was the last time someone had waved at her in LA?

Jenna's lips thinned. *Probably never.*

The sisters collided and embraced each other in the way people did when they shared hard news—long and tight, and as if they hadn't seen each other in a long time, which they hadn't.

"Thanks for getting here so quickly," Sarah said by way of greeting, rushing past pleasantries.

"I got here as soon as I could. How's Dad doing?" Aunt May, her father's sister, had been her dad's constant companion for the past several years, especially as her health had deteriorated. If anyone would feel her passing as acutely as Jenna, who'd grown up with the woman as a second mother, it would be her father.

Sarah exhaled, releasing Jenna from her grip as she did. "Stoic as ever, and slipping in jokes to cover up his emotions. He was having lunch with Aunt May when it happened."

"Really?" Jenna took in her sister's puffy eyes and knew she'd been crying. Sarah's dark hair was pulled back and she'd wrapped herself in a thick cardigan, unconcerned about the heat of the warm summer afternoon. Grief had a way of turning people cold, and a shiver ran through Jenna. "I'm so grateful she had him with her when…"

Emotions rolled through Jenna and her sister pulled her in for another hug. "Me too."

"I wish I'd been here to say goodbye," Jenna mumbled, mostly to herself, then sniffed back a fresh crop of tears. "I wasn't here for her birthday—"

"She knew you would have been if you could. Aunt May loved seeing you happy, and she knew how much your work meant to you."

Yeah, but it doesn't matter half as much, Jenna thought. "Work was the last thing May and I talked about. It all feels so trivial now."

"She was proud of you." Sarah attempted a smile, but it wilted at the edges. "Trust me, she was, and she never let anyone forget it, either. I think all of Maui knows about the mainland architectural adventures of Jenna Burke."

Hopefully May's version of the story was more impressive than Jenna's. "Where's Mike?" she asked.

"Picking up the kids."

"How are they handling this?"

Her sister pulled a face. "Ethan is addicted to video games and Emma's a teenager. They didn't really know Aunt May as well as … well … you know."

"Right." Jenna remembered her recent conversation with Patti about teenage years. It wasn't easy on anybody, especially parents. While one was trying to find their footing in a new world of young adulthood, the other was holding on to the past and worrying about them growing up too quickly.

As if his fatherly instincts had alerted him his daughters were talking about him, Jenna's father emerged from the house. His arms were spread wide in welcome to his younger daughter, though the smile on his face was pained, almost forced. Like Aunt May, he too looked older than when Jenna had him seen at the online birthday party. Maybe the camera added ten pounds, but took away a few years?

"Hi, Daddy."

Jim pulled her into a tight embrace. "*Aloha*, Peanut. I'm glad you're here."

"Are you okay?" she asked through the bulk of his arms. Jim Burke had always been a man of the island, tall and broad with long black hair and warm, kind eyes, but time and age had softened him. The firm muscles he'd had as a younger man had become spongier, though he was still as strong as ever and his dark hair still just as black, only now edged in silver. Hugging her dad was like squeezing a big teddy bear. The thought made her cling just a little longer to him than she otherwise might have, lingering in the cozy heat of his embrace, the smell of the ocean fresh on his skin.

"No. But you're not either, right?"

Jenna shook her head as her father turned to her sister. "Are you?"

The tears streaming down Sarah's face were so heavy they weighed down their father's voice. "Well, then ... bring it in here."

Sarah joined the hug, and for a moment the three stood there, arms around each other, each finding comfort in the other.

"I think us being together is a wonderful blessing," Jim said. "Don't you?"

Both girls nodded.

"Let's go inside."

Jim picked up Jenna's bag, and his eyes widened in surprise. There was a catch in his voice. "This bag isn't heavy enough, Peanut. I hope you're staying longer than last time."

"Just through the service, Dad."

The sadness in his expression stung. "I'm very busy at work," she added by way of apology.

He slung the lightweight bag over his shoulder with one arm and curved his lips upward into a smile. "There's always something to get back to, but I'll take as many moments as I can get. You girls are my aloha."

As Jenna followed her father and sister into the house, she thought back to the week before. How different life had been then. She and Darren had still been together, her upcoming pitch on Terrace Pines had still been full of potential, she'd never cried at work, and she'd still had Aunt May. At her birthday party, Jenna had watched on the screen as Aunt May beamed full of life, as if the illness she'd been fighting for so long had finally lost its hold on her. She'd laughed, eaten two slices of her favorite cake, a coconut-and-cream Hawaiian delicacy of Sarah's, and … "On her birthday, Aunt May asked if I still had Ruby," Jenna thought out loud.

"Your hammer?" Jim and Sarah asked at the same time. One's voice sounded as if she'd just said the name of a long-lost friend, the other, incredulous.

Nodding, Jenna thought back to when she'd worked alongside her dad and Aunt May on various construction projects. Her dad was always building something—it was probably how he'd managed to keep so strong in his later years. Nothing built muscle and stamina quite like swinging a hammer all day. Ruby had been a gift, emblazoned with the little red gems that gave the tool its namesake, given to Jenna when she was a girl and had started building with her dad. "I haven't seen it in years."

Sarah, who had never quite shared the family fondness for building things, had more recent relationships on her mind. "Where's Darren?" she asked, eyes narrowed.

Jim grunted under his breath. "Oh yeah, I forgot about ol' what's-his-name."

"Things have changed between me and what's-his-name." Jenna sighed and forced a definite yet ambivalent tone into her voice. "Please no follow-up questions."

"Hallelujah."

Sarah shook a scolding finger at her father, who'd clearly read between the lines. "Daddy, be nice."

"What?" Jim harrumphed. "Never much liked the guy. A man's hands need to have dirt on them. My own daughters can build a house from a hole in the ground and that man couldn't even hang drywall."

"Maybe Jenna can build a house, but I don't know the difference between a nail and a screw." Sarah scoffed and turned to her sister. "I'm sorry about you and Darren," she added, though she only sounded half-sorry.

Jenna got the impression her dad wasn't the only one who hadn't cared much for her ex. "It took me a long time to figure it out, but he turned out to be … well, not right for me."

"*Ho 'alo a ha'alele paha i ka ipu,*" Jim said with a smile. He wrapped his free arm around Jenna's shoulders and squeezed. "No better way to rid the world of louses than a little sunshine."

Jenna couldn't stop the smile that spread across her face at the mention of sunshine. Yeah, she was sunny. Even more important, she liked herself that way. Aunt May had, too, and her opinion mattered mountains more than Orville Barrington's or Darren Taylor's.

"Come on, let's get you settled," Sarah said, ushering her father and sister inside the house. She dropped her voice and winked at her sister. "Then you and I are gonna have some girl talk."

꙳

Sarah might not have known the finer points of hardware, but she definitely knew how to command an oven.

"These look absolutely amazing," Jenna gushed as her sister set down a large tray of pastries on the kitchen table while she sat sipping a steaming cup of butterscotch tea. She eyed the tray, amazed at her sister's creativity. Everything looked delicious and artisanal, almost too good to eat, but Jenna eyed a white-dusted lemon bar and felt her stomach grumble. "I forgot all about your confections. I don't know where to start."

"Just something I threw together," Sarah shrugged modestly.

"So, tell me everything. What happened with Darren?"

The girls turned to see their father hovering nearby.

"Dad, what part of girl talk includes *you*?" Sarah teased.

He motioned innocently at the spread of desserts on the table. "I gotta get back to working on my project, but I was just hoping to get myself one of those pastries."

The sisters watched as their father plucked a plate from the cupboard and stacked an assortment of sweets on the ceramic. He tucked an extra morsel between his teeth, just for good measure.

"*Mahalo*," he managed between bits of brownie as he made his way to the back door.

When the coast was clear, Sarah leaned in toward her sister. "Okay. Spill it."

Jenna shrugged. Really, there wasn't much to spill. Nothing her sister wouldn't already expect anyway. She decided to leave romantic financial investments out of it and get straight to the point. "After four years of dating, it seemed like we stopped growing as a couple."

"You do know *dating* for four years isn't really supposed to be a thing, don't you?"

"It's not?" Of course her *married* sister knew all about the rules of dating.

Sarah shot her a motherly look. "No. That's just sort of being a perpetual renter at love, but never getting your name on the mortgage."

Jenna smirked. How would Darren, Mr. Fancy Pants realtor, have liked her sister's metaphor? "That sounds like something Aunt May would have said. I guess we were kind of in a rut. We didn't kiss as often, and forgot to say, 'I love you' a lot."

"That's old married couple stuff. Trust me, I know." Sarah

held up a ring finger, displaying a gold wedding band topped with a princess-cut diamond. "But I got the ring. And the 'till death do us part.' That's what gets you through the ruts."

"I waited for him such a long time." Jenna sighed. "I just hate starting over."

"I know, but sometimes one step back is two steps forward."

"Now that's *definitely* Aunt May talking right there," Jenna said. She laughed, and the sound was sharp around the edges.

A beat of unexpected silence passed. Both women sipped at their tea in quiet thought.

"I'm going to miss her so much," Jenna said, finally.

"Me, too."

Jenna had just picked up a second lemon bar when the sound of the front door opening signaled new arrivals. A few footsteps later, Sarah's husband, Mike, appeared in the kitchen, loaded down with his children's belongings.

He deposited the clutter unceremoniously in a heap on the kitchen floor, then stooped to hug Jenna, adjusting his glasses so they didn't smudge against her cheek. "Hello, Jenna. Good to see you. I'm so sorry about Aunt May."

Jenna swallowed the lump of pastry and grief stuck in her throat. "Where are the kids?"

Mike rolled his eyes. "They went to their rooms to 'change,'" he explained, using air quotes the way parents sometimes did when they knew their children probably were doing anything other than what they were supposed to be doing. "They'll either be down in a bit to say hello—or we'll possibly never see them again. Where's Darren?"

Sarah shot her husband a look.

"What did I say?"

Sarah picked up a pastry and broke it in half, sending a clear message to her husband.

Mike caught it. He winced as he turned back to Jenna and looked as if he'd suddenly gotten a very bad toothache. "Got it. Well, good riddance to bad rubbish is what I always say."

Sarah banged the baking sheet again and mouthed *no* while Jenna pretended not to notice.

"This whole family speaks in riddles!" she said. "You guys *really* didn't like him, did you?"

Mike suppressed a shudder. "*Really, really.* Jen, you know you can stay as long as you want," he added, changing the subject.

"Thank you. I can stay through Aunt May's service, but then I have to get back. In addition to losing a boyfriend, I lost a big project. I have a lot of work to do to redeem myself."

Her sister gave her a rueful smile. "Then we'll just have to make an island girl out of you while we have you."

Chapter Eight

Sarah had arranged a memorial gathering for Aunt May the very next evening. Her ample sitting room was filled with framed photographs of May's life, showcasing precious moments of the family's timeline interspersed with platters of pastries she'd spent half the day and most of the night before baking. Tropical drinks had turned grief into celebration, and family and friends packed the rooms, some sporting Hawaiian shirts and flower leis as they chattered and mingled. It was a Maui-style wake, full of life and love.

E hele me ka pu'olo. Jenna remembered the meaning of the proverb. Make every person, place, or condition better than you left it.

"It's nice for everyone to be able to be together to celebrate May," she said, watching as two unfamiliar faces in a corner laughed loudly over a shared joke. Just because she didn't recognize everyone at the memorial didn't mean her Aunt May hadn't left her touch on everyone she met.

"Everybody on the island loved her," her sister agreed. "Good thing we didn't have to put the word out wide about the memorial. We would have had to rent out the Grand Wailea."

A cousin whose named escaped Jenna joined the throng. "Do you remember the summer Aunt May bought her old tractor? She was determined to conquer her own lawn care needs, no matter that her property was large enough to hire a four-man crew." He pointed at Jenna. "You must have been yea high." He hovered his palm in the air near his hips. "Said you'd help mow if she let you build a treehouse out in the big elm in the back."

"I remember," Jenna said. Aunt May had let her help, and she'd spent the rest of the summer drawing blueprints of her dream treehouse on every scrap of paper she could find. "She even let me ride that old tractor once or twice."

"As I remember, nobody could peel you off of it," Sarah teased. "You were just as determined to build your treehouse as Aunt May was to mow her lawn."

"Hey, it was my first official architectural project! Made me the woman I am." Jenna laughed.

Sarah gave her an appraising look, but before she could comment, Jim approached, a serious look stamped on his face. He tried to force a smile, but the look of exhaustion Jenna had noticed before seemed heavier now, weighting his body down with grief and sadness. Her dad was putting on a brave face for the good of the family, but the strain was taking a toll.

"If you'll excuse us just one minute," he said, gathering Jenna, Sarah, and Mike from the throng of well-wishers. "Grace wants to speak to May's immediate family."

Jenna arched an eyebrow, surprised to hear the name of the long-time family lawyer. "Grace Miller?"

"Grace is handling May's estate and she's leaving tomorrow. Like I said before, there's always somewhere to get back to. It's unfortunate timing, so we have to get things sorted out now."

A handsome woman made up of pearls and starched collars, Grace was waiting for the family in Sarah's study. The small, well-furnished room at the back of the house was meant to be used as a place of relaxation but had instead been overrun with the bric-a-brac of parenting two growing children. Sarah kept the room tidy, but evidence of her children was still there—a mismatched pair of Ethan's shoes, some of Emma's old surfing gear, half a dozen tattered textbooks, and a plush toy that had seen better days. Besides the kitchen, the study was the only room in the house that looked truly lived in. Of course, with Grace Miller in it, any room would look disheveled. Not only was she one of those women who never seemed to age, but she had the look of someone who could frighten wrinkles right off her face.

She's an older version of Patti, Jenna mused. Both women were blonde, and both knew how to command a room, but where Patti's confidence was borne of wit and cleverness, Grace could charm your socks right off your feet without even trying—and then send you the bill for dry cleaning.

"I apologize for interrupting the memorial but thank you all so much for taking a moment away to have a short word about May's estate." Grace welcomed the family to the room as if it were her own, extending her long, slender arms to shake hands and dole out quick, perfunctory hugs. Someone, presumably Sarah, had cleared a section of clutter from the small coffee table in the center of a ring of sitting furniture, and Grace arranged her papers importantly on the table's surface as she waited for the family to settle around her. "May expressed her desire on a speedy resolution of her will because she knew how hard it would be to get the whole family together in one place."

There was the hint of an insinuation in Grace's words and Jenna's cheeks burned as she fought to keep her face neutral. So what if she was the only one who'd left the island to pursue her dreams in California? Was leaving home really such a crime?

"May had very little in the way of earthly treasures to leave behind," Grace continued. "Her only real asset was her house and the land it's on, which, of course, is worth more than the structure. What money she did leave is to be used to renovate the home."

The heat in Jenna's cheeks cooled. Aunt May's house had been a second home to her when she was growing up, even if it had always been too big for one woman to care for. Her thoughts raced through memories of playing in the flower gardens at the edge of May's property. She and Sarah stampeding down the house's large staircase and into the kitchen for breakfast on weekend mornings. Watching sunsets over the ocean horizon from the back porch.

"May loved that old place. What a wonderful project it'll be for you to restore, Dad," she said.

Grace fingered the pearl necklace strung around her slender neck. "Actually, May had something else in mind." A smile tugged at the corner of her lips. "She left the house, and thus all of her assets, to Jenna and Sarah."

Sarah and Jenna stared dumbfounded at each other for the space of a few breaths. Jenna had to blink a few times before she was sure she'd heard Grace right.

"The house?" they both echoed.

"The place is a wreck!" Sarah added.

Jim cleared his throat. "Sarah!"

Sarah spread her hands out before her. "Sorry, Dad. But after Aunt May moved into the retirement home … the house sort of fell apart."

Unfamiliar tension filled the space between her father and her sister, and Jenna cut in before it could implode. "Ms. Miller, did Aunt May say what she wanted us to do with the property? Are we supposed to sell it?"

"How could we even consider selling it?" Jim's voice was thick with emotion. "She was like a mother to you girls after your mom passed, and May's house is all we have left of her now."

"But it's a *house*," Sarah argued. "And it's a *lot* of house. We can't just—"

Grace stacked her papers sharply on the desk, capturing the family's attention. "To answer your question, Jenna—" She cut her eyes at Jim, and then Sarah. "*If* you decide to sell the house, then she wanted you and your sister to split the proceeds. But, there is one condition."

A condition? Jenna blinked. "What?"

"If you girls want to sell the house, Jenna has to renovate it first."

The sisters shared another surprised look. This time, Jim joined.

"Renovate the house?" Jenna shifted her gaze from Sarah to Grace and back. She didn't have time for this. Taking a few days off to mourn and handle family matters was one thing, but Patti would expect her back in the office pronto. There were designs to finish, pitches to perfect, clients to land. Dreams to achieve. She could pause her life in the city for a day or two, but a month wouldn't be nearly long enough to revive her Aunt May's estate. Not even close. "I live in Los Angeles. Taking time off to stay in Maui and renovate May's house isn't exactly in the plan."

Grace gave her a patient, if a tiny bit condescending, smile.

"I'm afraid May's will is rather specific. You have to supervise the work. Otherwise, the house cannot be sold."

Jenna swung her gaze back to Sarah for help, who shrugged. "If you think about it … it's kind of the perfect plan, Jen. You're an amazing architect and designer."

Jenna huffed. "What's not perfect is I have a job twenty-five hundred miles away I have to get back to. Aunt May knew that, too. I don't understand what she was thinking. Renovating her house could take weeks. Months." She shot her eyes to her sister. "Why not Sarah?"

Sarah bristled beside her, and Jenna hoped she hadn't taken umbrage. Just because Sarah was a full-time stay-at-home mom didn't mean she wasn't busy with her own life, although Jenna couldn't imagine what could possibly occupy her time.

"Seriously, Jenna? I do spatulas, not hammers. I wouldn't know the first thing about renovations, not even enough to supervise. That's all you."

Though Sarah hadn't said it, Jenna heard the implied, "And Dad." The sisters had danced around the divide between them—how Jenna had been a daddy's girl with her hammers and tools while Sarah had been closer to their mother and her love of baking—but never had it seemed so stark as it suddenly did at this moment. It would seem Aunt May's house wasn't the only thing in need of a bit of renovation, but Jenna hardly had time to think about her relationship with her sister now.

"I haven't held a hammer in years," she said, hoping to ward off her sister's ever-tightening glare. "I don't understand, Grace."

Grace slipped her papers back inside her leather portfolio and closed it with an authoritative *snap*. "Regardless, these are May's wishes. The will says once Jenna's done with the work, you girls can do whatever you want with the house. Rent it. Sell it. Live in it. Your choice."

Jenna rose from the couch to pace the length of the small room. How was she possibly going to deal with this? Perhaps her aunt had put too much faith in her. After all, she couldn't even sell her own ideas—how was she going to live up to May's? "But—"

"Jenna," Grace interrupted. She lifted a hand into the air as if her delicate wrist and five slender fingers could ward off the hundreds of questions and contingencies already queuing up in Jenna's mind. "In my very first case, a man left his prized possession—a 1957 Chevy—to his youngest, thirty-year-old, unemployed son who didn't even have a driver's license. His three other grown sons did, and by all accounts were successful men who loved cars. We were all scratching our heads, but within a few weeks the youngest son had his driver's license and applied for a job so he could make money to maintain the car. He's been driving that car around town ever since."

"Mr. Hayes?" Jenna asked, thinking of the older gentleman a few years ahead of her father's age who'd driven by when she'd arrived yesterday morning. Everyone who'd grown up on the island knew the old man and his car. It didn't matter what time of year it was—he was always out and about in the old Chevy.

"That's right. And the car looks as good as it did the day he got it. The point is, there's a reason May left things the way she did. A will is a request—a way for those who have passed to affect those who live on."

With a sigh, Jenna sat back down and resisted the urge to wring her hands. She really needed to get back to the city, but she also didn't want to disappoint Aunt May—or dishonor her last request.

Thanks, Aunt May. It didn't look like she had any options. At least it was a renovation, not a reconstruct. A renovation wasn't a new build and it didn't require her usual attention to architectural design, but it was a job—and all jobs had a finish line. They also needed a team. "I'll need help finding a contractor."

Grace's lips tightened into a line, as if she were biting back a secret. "That's already been taken care of. Your aunt was very specific about whom she wanted to assist you with the renovation."

Electricity prickled along Jenna's skin, causing little goose bumps to rise along her flesh. She was the architect here. The contractor should be her choice. "What if I don't like him?"

"May was always a good judge of character," Jim assured her. He laid a finger on Jenna's arm, smoothing away the goosebumps. "She was right about Darren," he added knowingly.

"Aunt May didn't like Darren either?" The empty space on Jenna's ring finger went cold. Apparently, her whole family had disapproved of her ex, but all had seen fit to let her figure it out on her own. Was she really so hard-headed—or had she just not been paying attention?

There was mischief in her father's eyes. "She would never tell you herself, but she knew he was no good."

"So, what are you going to do?" asked Sarah from Jenna's side. Her sister's voice was devoid of the soft warmth their father's had. Instead, her tone was cold and hard, and more than a little impatient.

"It's Aunt May's last wish," Jenna relented. "I don't really have a choice."

Grace slid a piece of paper across the coffee table to Jenna to sign, acknowledging her aunt's will had been shared and she understood the conditions of her inheritance. She signed.

Chapter Nine

"I don't get it. Why would Aunt May leave me a giant, dilapidated house I wouldn't be able to live in even if it were livable?"

Jenna had slept on Grace's surprise news, and yet Aunt May's last wishes still hadn't become any clearer. *Slept on is a bit of an exaggeration*, she thought. It was true. In fact, Jenna had barely slept at all, her mind too busy to relax, much less fall asleep, with all the questions she wished she had answers for piling up. She'd spent half the night tossing and the other half turning, and by the time the sun had peeked over the horizon, Jenna had already been on her third cup of tea in her sister's kitchen and was still just as confused in the morning sun as she'd been when she went to bed the night before.

"It just doesn't make any sense," she continued, looping Sarah into the conversation as her sister made her way into the kitchen. Her sister dropped into the chair across from Jenna with a yawn.

"No matter how I try to puzzle it out, I can't figure out why May would leave us the house. No," she corrected. "I guess *leaving* us the house I can understand, but why require we fix it up before selling it?" Jenna shook her head and moved on to cup number four, draining what was left in the kettle into her teacup. She reached for the sugar bowl and scooped another heaping spoonful into her mug. At this point, she needed all the energy she could get, even if it came with a bunch of unnecessary calories. "Why put so much energy—and so much hassle—into something neither one of us plans to keep? It just seems like a monumental waste of time and resources."

"She loved her house." Sarah's voice was still thick from sleep as she mumbled through a second yawn. She stretched and yawned again, then reached for the kettle and attempted to pour herself a mug. Empty. Shooting her sister the evil eye, Sarah pushed herself up from the table and shambled to the sink to refill the pot. "Remember, you and Dad would be over there all the time fixing stuff up. Aunt May liked it in top condition, but with a house that size—and age—it was a lot even back then, and that doesn't even take into consideration the rest of the property. With you gone and Dad getting older, the house and everything else kind of fell into disrepair, especially after we talked her into moving into the assisted living center."

Sarah paused, considering, and her face darkened. "I'm sure Aunt May felt the house deserved better, like she wanted everyone's memory of her home to be like it used to be. Maybe she thought being the architect in the family, fixing it up would mean something to you."

Jenna followed the sugar by adding a little more cream into her mug, hoping it would take away the bitterness clinging to the roof of her mouth. The way Sarah spoke, it sounded like she was blaming her ... but what for? Moving to the city? Living her life elsewhere while Sarah was still in the suburbs, taking care of their dad on top of her own family? For not being around to look after Aunt May's house?

She avoided Sarah's gaze as her sister dropped into her chair across the table. The last thing Jenna wanted to do was argue. Not now, not right after losing Aunt May. And not coming off a night of no sleep. "May wants me to do the renovation, but she left the house to both of us. You're part of this, too. We could use your help."

"You think it was easy for me?" The sound of sleep was gone from Sarah's voice. "I felt left out when you and Dad went off to work on her house. Always just the two of you. Not me."

Jenna's shoulders tightened. "Why didn't you come? You were always welcome."

Sarah shrugged, sipping from the mug she'd brought back to the table with her. "Because it wasn't for me, really. I never saw the fun in all that banging and painting and sawing. I just wanted to be included, I guess. It was easier for me to stay back with Mom. Being with her in the kitchen was how I discovered my thing, even if it didn't exactly amount to anything special."

"Baking." Tears stung behind Jenna's eyes. Growing up, Jenna had gotten all the time with their dad and Aunt May, but Sarah had been closer to their mom. Jenna had always envied the relationship her older sister had with their mother, and after Nancy Burke had passed away, Jenna had always thought she'd never really gotten to know her mom—not like Sarah had. Jenna had been a teenager, but Sarah had already headed off to college and taking years' worth of memories with her that Jenna had never had time to make. She'd never considered how Sarah might envy the relationship she'd built with their father and aunt in the same way Jenna had Sarah's relationship with their mother. Apparently, they'd both envied what the other had.

"Do you know why I used to love to go over there and help Dad fix stuff?" Jenna asked.

Sarah shook her head, hiding her expression behind a sip of tea.

"Because Aunt May always made cookies and lemonade. It was all about the cookies and lemonade. You got that gift from her and Mom, not me."

An unexpected smirk pushed the shadows out of her sister's face. "And it's just a coincidence you eventually became an incredibly successful architect while I became a stay-at-home mom and home baker."

Jenna clicked her tongue. "An architect, yes. But I don't know about the incredible part—or successful."

"Why would you say that?"

"I presented a project the other day for a luxury condominium. It was perfect. I did everything right, gave the potential investor everything they asked for and more. I poured my *soul* into the concept. But in the end, they went with a competing proposal. Want to know why?"

It felt good to get this out, to share the disaster that was Terrace Pines and Orville Barrington with someone other than people who had a vested interest in the project. No matter how supportive Patti had been, at the end of the day she was still Jenna's boss, not her friend. She'd tell Jenna to work harder, that losing deals happened every day, but none of it really made her feel any better. Kind of made her feel worse, actually. She wasn't sure how she felt about having to work so hard only to face the possibility of constant disappointment.

At least you don't have Darren's opinion to worry about anymore. The thought burned.

"Will it make me angry?" Sarah asked, big sister voice fully engaged.

"Furious," Jenna promised. "After I pitched, a competing firm came in ten percent under budget. I was only five. *Five* percent under, instead of ten. But my proposal would have saved them a ton of money down the line—far more than a lousy extra five percent. The little bit of difference upfront would have been pennies in the bucket the first time they looked at a balance sheet. Didn't matter. The investors had absolutely no foresight, just looked at the number and walked."

"You're right, that's ridiculous," her sister agreed. "You'd think investors would be more interested in long-term earnings than making a quick buck."

"You'd think."

"I'm sorry, Jen." There was a pause. "You never told me about the cookies and lemonade."

Jenna sighed. "The moral of the story is that spending all that time with Dad and Aunt May working on the house helped me grow into who I am, even if I'm still working to achieve my particular dream. Maybe it's the same way for you—you have so much talent. I think you could make a brick taste like heaven." She paused to consider her words, and her stomach rumbled. "I miss Mom's blondies."

Sarah smiled for the first time that morning. "They were one of my favorites too. I know the recipe by heart. I'll make them for you."

"You would? Thanks."

Sarah sniffed. "You're going to need every advantage you can get. You have your work cut out for you with Aunt May's house."

"So, I take it you're not coming along this time either? I can teach you how to swing a hammer."

"Oh, not a chance," Sarah shot back. "You renovate. I'll keep you stocked with baked goods and sugar."

"The house can't be that bad," Jenna wondered aloud. "Can it?"

❋

Apparently, it could. In fact, the condition of Aunt May's once-beautiful home was worse than Jenna could have imagined. She had expected the home to need a bit of maintenance, a definite scrub and shine, but this...

"Wow." Jenna stopped beside her sister in front of Aunt May's home and stared. If she hadn't been looking at the house with her own eyes, she'd never have believed it. May's house wasn't a home anymore. It was a ruin.

Sarah exhaled a deep sigh and grabbed Jenna's hand, pulling her onward. "Told you."

Jenna had a hard time putting her thoughts into words as she let herself be led up the rickety front steps. What she remembered as a sprawling Victorian with vibrant paint, delicate gingerbread trim, and curling ivy that crawled up front steps to wide double doors was now a ramshackle heap with peeling paint, gaping shutters, and slanted steps. The wooden wraparound porch was missing planks and several windows were either cracked or broken. Most of the trim was gone. The garden was weeds.

So much for curb appeal. Any hope Jenna had of fixing this place up quick and getting it on the market evaporated. The house didn't so much need renovation as it did a total overhaul. Best case scenario, they'd have to gut and redo. Worst case ... she didn't want to think about worst case. Her dad might faint if she so much as breathed the word *demolition*—not to mention Aunt May would haunt her dreams forever.

"If you listen really carefully, you can hear the structure groaning," Sarah said.

Jenna noticed a crack in the section of roof overhanging the porch. "No, that's me *actually* groaning."

"It's not so bad. Some new windows and a coat of paint, and you're in business."

Jenna rolled her eyes. Now she knew why her sister was so quick to volunteer to stay home and make blondies. "You mean *we're* in business."

Sarah wasn't having it. "Oh, no. I told you, I don't do hard labor. I've never even picked up a hammer in my life—that was always your thing, and Dad and Mike have saved me from a lifetime of manual labor ever since. I don't even know which end of the hammer is the part you hold, and which is the part you slam down on the screw."

Jenna gave her sister an exasperated look. "Don't get carried away with hyperbole, Sarah. Anyone who's ever seen a hammer knows which is the business end, and I'm pretty sure you've seen a hammer. I don't bake, and even I know there's one on the cover of every box of *Arm & Hammer* baking soda."

Her sister lifted her hands, protesting ignorance. "All I'm saying is I have two teens at home who need more attention than the average toddler. This is all you, sister."

Jenna was about to reply that *she* also had responsibilities which required her attention, but just as she readied to do so, a gray pickup truck rumbled up the gravel drive. *Legacy Renovations* was stenciled on the side in blue, along with a phone number bearing the local area code.

Sarah sensed an opportunity. "That must be the contractor. I should go. Good luck."

Her sister was halfway down the steps before Jenna could respond. The pickup's door squealed on its hinges, grating directly against Jenna's nerves.

"Thanks," she muttered to her sister's back. "I'm going to need it."

Jenna wrinkled her nose. Luck. Patti had said the same thing to her the day of the Terrace Pines pitch. Hopefully the old saying was true—lightning never strikes the same place twice.

Chapter Ten

Jenna watched from the sagging front porch of Aunt May's Victorian as a man opened the driver's side door and slid out of the pickup. He waved in greeting and she lifted her hand in reply, then sucked in a deep breath. Hopefully this was the guy Grace had mentioned and not some opportunist who'd happened to drive by and see two women standing in front of a crumbling house and looking completely out of their element.

Then you'd *be the curb appeal,* she thought and snorted. She took another look at the guy walking up the drive and revised her opinion. Whoever he was, contractor or busybody Good Samaritan, he rocketed right past curb appeal and landed directly on curb *candy.*

Jenna tried not to notice how the guy's toolbelt hung low on his hips and swung when he walked, or how the thin cotton of his T-shirt bunched and rippled over his chest as he strode toward her—his dishwater blond hair that gleamed like gold in the sun. He certainly *looked* like a contractor with his clipboard and rolled-up blueprints tucked under one very-muscular arm, but had she ever seen a contractor who looked like this before? *Definitely not.* If she had, she'd have spent more time out in the field and less in front of her drafting table.

The guy nodded at Jenna and his eyes swept from her to the

house. "Absolutely beautiful, isn't she?"

"Are we looking at the same house?" Jenna asked. She squinted in the bright afternoon sun and lifted a hand to shield her gaze. "And how do you know it's a she?"

He climbed up the front steps and ran his fingers down a place where the trim had come detached from the frame and splintered. "Just look at her," he instructed, a note of reverence in his voice. "This house is a beautiful old soul. She has given so much of herself she appears to have almost nothing left, but that couldn't be further from the truth."

He turned the full weight of his gaze on Jenna, and she swallowed down her reaction to his stunning Hawaiian sky blue eyes and perfect stubble as he took a step closer. He inspected a crack in the window, tapping at it gently with his fingertip.

"She may be a little broken, but she still stands strong. We have to remind her of what she's capable of and who she is, the beauty and strength that still lies within. That she deserves better."

What? His last words breathed across her skin, and Jenna had to blink a few times before she found her voice. "Are you a contractor or a poet?" Her voice came out husky.

The guy grinned, unabashed. He stuck out a hand. "Ben Fletcher, *Legacy Renovations*. You must be Jenna. Your aunt told me all about you."

Jenna accepted a quick squeeze but pulled back her hand before it got too comfortable. His grip felt like a warm bath—a warm bath with a pulse. "She did?"

Ben nodded as if it was the most natural thing in the world for an old woman to be dishing on her niece to the stranger to whom she'd decided to entrust her home's renovations after her death. "She spoke very highly of you. I'm sorry for your loss."

"Did you know Aunt May well?"

"I used to help out with small fixes. I always wanted to do more work on the house, but May wouldn't let me. I didn't understand why at the time." He winked. "But it makes sense now."

Well what on earth did that mean? *It doesn't matter*, Jenna decided. They had a job to do, and if Aunt May had decided this was the guy she wanted to trust, then that was good enough for her. "I'm glad it makes sense to someone. Aunt May left me the house and I have to fix it up."

Ben crooked an eyebrow. "You *have* to? You don't *want* to?"

This conversation seemed to be heading into deeper subjects than Jenna was in the mood to entertain. She sighed. "It's in the will and I live in Los Angeles. I have a job and a boyfriend—" She stopped herself, readjusted. "Or at least I *had* a boyfriend. My point is, I don't have time for this in my life right now."

Ben gave her a look as if he found her explanation more entertaining than convincing. "Maybe you're not living the right life, then. Let's head inside and see what we're up against."

※

As depressing as the outside of the house was, the inside was worse. Time had wreaked havoc on the exterior, but for all the bluster of wind and elements that had made their mark on Aunt May's once-grand home, a different sort of aging had befallen the inside. This one had been slow and thorough. It had dulled the wallpaper. Buckled the crown molding with water damage. Wrapped itself in dusty cobwebs across every surface and down every threshold. Even the air smelled of loneliness and neglect.

A loose floorboard cracked under Jenna's feet as she stepped across the threshold. She lost her footing as the hardwood gave out beneath her and braced herself for a rough landing. Before she could get her hands out in front of her, Jenna found herself swept up in Ben's arms, staring into the little specks of gold around his pupils. Dimples hid beneath the layer of stubble on his jaw, and freckles decorated the space under his eyes and across the bridge of his nose. Sun-kissed.

Sunny. Jenna hid her blush behind a look of defiance as she removed herself from Ben's arms and righted herself on a sturdier area of flooring. She tried to force the appropriate words of gratitude through her lips, but they got stuck in her throat. This was a consult, not a date. *Stick to business, Jenna.*

She pulled down the hem of her tank top. "Thank you."

Ben bit back a grin as he scratched a note on his clipboard. "Okay, the floor might be a good place to start. The hardwood is original. I can match the boards with engineered wood if there aren't too many that need to be replaced. Refinish the rest."

"I'm sure we can salvage most of them. The original floors and fixtures are part of the house's charm." Charm might have been a strong word, but repurposing original materials was not only sustainable but trendy. Plus, using what you already had saved time and money. Jenna took another step farther into the house. Beneath her, another board creaked.

She froze. Salvaging wouldn't be possible if she broke every floorboard on the first walk-through.

"Maybe I'll go first."

Ben's attempt at chivalry earned him a sharp glare from Jenna, but she gestured him forward. He took a step and another floorboard cracked. When Ben's arm flung out, Jenna caught it, preventing him from earning a trip to first base with the wooden floor.

"Great plan."

"You're right. Maybe we should sit and scoot instead."

Jenna swallowed a laugh. It would be funny if it wasn't so terribly, terribly true. So much for salvaging.

Things weren't any better when they arrived in the kitchen on tiptoe. Cabinet doors hung from their hinges and the linoleum tiling had begun to curl and peel away from the floor. Jenna tried the faucet over the kitchen sink and muddy brown sludge gurgled forth. She recoiled. The thick liquid not only looked gross but had an unpleasant odor too.

Ben made another note on his clipboard. "New kitchen. Probably new plumbing."

"We need some new hardware, but the cabinet wood is still good, and a new washer should fix the faucet. Use what we have first. The linoleum goes, though. Let's put down laminate."

Ben rolled his gaze up from his clipboard to give Jenna a considering look.

"What?"

"Flooring I get, but I figured you'd want to rip all this out, replace it with new." He motioned to the fixtures and dropping cabinet. "We can source vintage."

"Sourcing requires time and research. Not to mention a larger than necessary budget for something that looks real, but isn't," she replied. "Part of what makes this house special is its history. You're the one who said she was a beautiful old soul and deserved to keep her beauty and strength intact. If we can't keep it, we replace it with something better, not try to fake it."

"You're right—I did say that, but we should give her a bit of a makeover along the way." Ben tapped the tip of his pencil against his clipboard, then tucked it behind his ear. He pointed at the window that ran along the side of the kitchen's breakfast nook, narrating as he swept his arm toward the adjacent dining room. "We can double the size of the eastern-facing window to allow more natural light inside—put in a whale window so we can bring in a view of the ocean, too. In the morning, the kitchen will light up like the dawn. Then we'll knock down this wall"—he gestured at the short pony wall separating the rooms. "And put in a nice big island. It'll be perfect. What do you think?"

Jenna considered Ben's vision. Old Victorians had notoriously closed floor plans, sectioning off the available square footage into small squares that interrupted the flow of the house. A more open floor plan would let the house breathe, and a whale window would provide a breathtaking view of the water—but taking down a wall and opening up a larger window space was a whole project unto itself. The designer in her approved. The organizer did not. "Let's put a pin in the idea and reevaluate once we know where things stand."

Ben made a note on his clipboard, and they moved on, circumventing more dodgy floorboards as they inspected the rest of the rooms on the bottom floor of the house.

Ben peeked his head in the lower guest bath. "New bathroom?"

"What? Why?" She cast a look around the small washroom. Of the three in the house, this little alcove beneath the stairs had been her favorite when she'd stayed with her aunt as a girl. Of course, it didn't look the same now as it had then, but the memories were still as fresh as ever. Aunt May had kept a small looking glass on the vanity. Jenna would study her reflection in the mirror and pretend she was a princess.

A pang of loss thumped in her chest. The mirror was gone now, along with almost everything else she remembered about the space.

"I see a wood-look tile—dark wood—and wainscot on the wall about three feet high. Maybe a rustic red paint above that, a walk-in shower, and dual sinks. A lot of potential here," Ben continued.

When Jenna shot a curious look his direction, he laughed. "I love bathrooms."

"That's a really weird thing to say." Weird, but endearing.

He shrugged, unfazed. "I do some of my best thinking in the shower. Some of my most important work is done before I ever get dressed in the morning. People spend more time than you realize in their bathrooms."

"It just needs to be a place to, you know, take care of business," Jenna argued, just for the sake of being disagreeable. "Let's not spend too much time or money on it."

Ben wrote a second note on his clipboard.

The two had their real first disagreement on the back porch.

"We have to replace this porch," Ben said.

Jenna groaned. "I see a pattern here." They'd been through the entire house, all two stories and thirteen rooms. During their inspection, Jenna's wishful thinking of getting the house up to marketable condition in any reasonable timeframe had dissolved under the reality of a complete gutting. She had taken small comfort in the hope she could repurpose many of the house's original features and save some money as well as preserve the home's historic charm. Unfortunately, Ben had wasted no breath pointing out every flaw and fix he saw, along with sharing a list of his ideas. Time and dollar signs stacked up in Jenna's mind, and her mixed priorities made her eyes cross. The architect in her wanted to focus on design and sustainability. The rest of her wanted to get out from under the house so she could get back to her life.

Ben was still going on about the back porch. "We'll build it with PVC—polyvinyl chloride. It has the look of wood, but it's not affected by weather like wood. We can even build a grill into the deck for a few dollars more since we're redoing from scratch. Extra function plus curb appeal."

Curb appeal. Jenna flinched. "I know what PVC is," she snapped. "Let's just tear the whole porch down and put some steps at the door."

"Steps?"

"There will be more backyard space that way."

Ben scratched at his temple. His face screwed up in confusion as if she'd just told him she wanted to build a space station in the backyard. "There's acres of land back here. You don't need more backyard space. You need a place to sit down with the family and share food and embarrassing stories. Maybe a little swing where a couple can come and sit after dinner and watch the sun go down."

Romantic, but impractical. "That's west," Jenna said, pointing to the front of the house. "The sun rises in front of the house."

"So, maybe before breakfast, then. You could sit out here and watch the sunrise."

Jenna sighed. "Wasn't that the point of widening the window in the kitchen?"

Ben scowled. He tapped his pencil against his clipboard. "Well, yes. But people do eat more than one meal a day, you know. It's not exactly a fast-paced life out here on the islands. Function is every bit as important as aesthetic. We're rebuilding a home, not a commercial space."

Aesthetics? Jenna knew all about the price of aesthetics. Something bitter landed on her tongue. She chewed at the inside of her cheek. "No porch. Just steps."

Without waiting for Ben's response, Jenna spun on her heel and headed back inside the house, arriving in the family room. She paused until his footsteps caught up behind her, then pointed an imperious finger at the fireplace. "Cover that up and box it in. Nobody needs a fireplace in Hawaii."

"Box it in?" Ben's voice was incredulous, bordering on angry. "The fireplace is one of the most unique features in the entire house. You want to make it disappear? Look at the character in the brick."

Jenna saw something, but it wasn't character. "You mean the cracks."

"I mean the *character*."

A floorboard groaned under Jenna, and heat flared in her cheeks. What was the point in trying to salvage a structure that so desperately wanted to fall apart around her? "Cover it and throw some laminate flooring down." A few more heartbeats' worth of hard stares passed, but Jenna wasn't backing down.

Neither was Ben. "This is a solid oak floor." His words came out careful and slightly condescending, with little pauses of frustration between. "The boards in this room are in good shape. Maybe we'll have to replace a few, but they're easy to match with engineered wood. With a sander and a nice finish, it'll pop like new. You can't put laminate over a floor like this."

The heat from Jenna's cheeks was coursing up her arms. She hadn't asked to renovate Aunt May's house, but this was the first design she'd had total control over, and she was going to take it. Then Barrington, Darren, and even Patti could see what she was capable of. Not only would she have this house polished up and ready for sale ahead of schedule, but she'd make sure to get it done under budget too. Take *that* ten percent.

"Sure, we can," she fired back. "Laminate looks like real wood but is more durable. And more cost effective."

Ben's eyebrows knit together. He cracked his neck. Said nothing.

"Go with a dark finish," Jenna decided. "We'll keep the walls light. Old world charm with a contemporary spin. Steel and brass finishes throughout." She turned her back on Ben, reconsidering the rooms above her head. She'd hoped to leave the upstairs hardwood, too, but a lot of people preferred a softer flooring where they slept. "And carpet for the bedrooms."

A sharp clang behind her let her know Ben had dropped his clipboard.

"*Carpet?*"

"I don't want any walls knocked down other than what we already agreed upon," Jenna continued as she made her way to the front door, not bothering to wait for Ben to catch up with her this time. "It's too time consuming. If anything, we can put in more windows to let in more natural light, but get my approval before you do anything. Otherwise, that should do it."

She held out her hand to shake on the deal, but Ben kept his arms pinned to his side. "I'm sorry. I'm not the guy for this job."

Jenna took a deep breath. "What? What do you mean? It's a job. It's a job with a big budget."

"And it should be done right," Ben replied. "But you're not interested in doing it right. And I'm not interested in doing it wrong."

This wasn't a moral debate. "It should be done my way—it's *my* house. My budget."

Ben crooked an eyebrow, and even his dimples seemed to be frowning. "On paper, sure. But you have no intention of keeping this house, or do you?"

"No." The word was sour. Jenna crossed her arms.

"So, it's a flip and that's fine, but it should still be done right. *Someone* is going to live here, maybe raise a family here." He took a meaningful step backward, giving Jenna the full measure of his gaze. "I told you, your aunt told me all about you."

Jenna scoffed. What was that supposed to mean?

"I know you're an architect," Ben explained, eyes flashing. "And I don't doubt for a second you pour every ounce of energy and love you have into the projects you work on. So why not put the same effort and care into this house? Doesn't your aunt deserve that—don't *you*?"

Ben's eyes bored holes into Jenna's, and it was she who broke the staring contest first, shifting her gaze out the window. "Look, I didn't ask to be put in this situation. If it were up to me, I'd put the house on the market and let the new owners make renovation decisions on their own. My job is to design new buildings, not heal broken ones."

"May made it sound like you loved this house. I guess she was wrong."

Jenna kept her gaze focused outside. She was still staring out the window when she heard Ben sigh and walk away.

Chapter Eleven

W ith the kids out of the house and her husband at work, Sarah had spent most of the day thinking... and baking. It was how she filled most of her days. With her kids growing up, Sarah's family seemed to need her less and less. It gave her more time to herself, something she'd have paid dearly for just a few years prior, but now that she had it, she didn't have a clue what to do with it.

Guess the grass is always greener, Sarah thought with a sigh. Most of the other women in her circle of friends—many of whom she'd come to know from the kids' sports activities, PTA events, and school functions—had found new ways to occupy their time, but Sarah hadn't. Not yet. So, she baked, played hide and seek with every speck of dust she could find lurking around the baseboards of her home, and cooked large family dinners nobody ate.

"May I be excused?" asked Emma. She'd been poking at her uneaten dinner for the past fifteen minutes.

When had Sarah's sweet-if-precocious little girl turned into the impatient sixteen-year-old across from her? "You didn't say two words over dinner."

Emma stabbed at a carrot. "Marley was supposed to text me. I have to check my phone."

Sarah glanced at Mike. He shrugged. *So much for backup.* "Okay, fine. Go."

Emma's fork clattered against her plate and her chair legs scraped against the tile as she shoved up and darted from the table. Ethan jumped up as well, like one of those little fish pulled along in the wake of a larger predator.

"Whoa, buddy, where are you going?"

Ethan shoved another dinner roll in his mouth. "I'm in the middle of a game of *Rebel Attack*," he mumbled around the bread. "If Emma can be dismissed, then I want to go, too."

Sarah sighed. "Did you do your homework?"

"Not completely—"

Big surprise. "Finish your homework and *then* you can play your video game."

"Mom!"

Her fourteen-year-old son's voice may have already cracked into puberty, but when he whined, he still sounded like a little boy. "Don't *Mom* me, just do it."

"Okay, okay," Ethan acquiesced, stuffing his pockets with more rolls before vanishing into the family room.

Sarah groaned and leaned back in her chair. "He really has to find an interest besides video games," she groused. "Books, sports, *something.* Video games are all he seems to care about these days."

"I know." Mike was already up and clearing the table, shepherding plates from the dining room table to the kitchen sink. This was an old argument. Sarah would complain about Emma's general lack of enthusiasm on anything involving family. She would insist Ethan needed a more constructive hobby to occupy his time. Mike would agree on both accounts but offer little in terms of a solution. Then Sarah would get aggravated until, eventually, the conversation turned from frustration about their children's lack of interest in anything that didn't involve a screen and end with them finding something to nitpick each other about. There was no sense in going down this familiar path tonight; it wouldn't lead anywhere she hadn't already been. Instead, watching Mike clear away dishes of the dinner she'd spent the better half of the afternoon preparing, Sarah thought perhaps her son wasn't the only one who needed a new hobby.

"Why do I cook?" she asked, watching as Emma's plate of uneaten food was swept from the table. "Why do I even bother?"

"I like your cooking," Mike responded automatically.

He'd been the only one to make a dent in his plate, but then Mike rarely met a meal he didn't like.

"I know you do, and I appreciate that."

"And your dad will be in the refrigerator later to polish off anything we didn't finish," Mike teased. "You know he will."

"He could just as easily join during family dinnertime instead of working on secret projects in the garage." At least her father could be counted on to make sure nothing Sarah cooked went uneaten.

Sarah reflected on her conversation with Jenna. If her sister was still working on putting the gift she'd earned from their family into action, then why couldn't she? Maybe she could turn her baking hobby into something more meaningful.

Speak of the devil. The front door opened, and Sarah's gaze swept to the small digital readout on the stove. Half past six. She'd left Jenna at Aunt May's early in the afternoon to meet with the contractor Grace had sent. Sarah had thought Jenna would be back in time for dinner to update her on the condition of the house. Was it a good sign that she'd been gone so long, or a bad one?

"That's Jenna," Sarah said, rising from the table. "I'll be back for the dishes. Thanks for putting everything away."

Mike smiled. "I'll clean up. Go talk to your sister."

❧

Jenna's day had gone from bad to worse. Not only was Aunt May's house in worse shape than she'd anticipated, now she had to find a way to break the news to Sarah that her aunt's chosen contractor had declined to take the job. Fulfilling Aunt's May wishes wasn't going to be easy without Ben—not that fulfilling them *with* Ben would have been any easier. She'd have to wait until Grace was back from her trip to New York to figure out what to do next, but first she had to face her sister.

"Why the long face?" Sarah asked as Jenna pulled up a seat at the dinner table.

"I hope I'm not disturbing your Friday night with your family."

Sarah slid a tray of uneaten pastries in front of Jenna. Blondies, just like she'd promised. "Not at all. After Mike cleans up after dinner, he'll disappear into his study, Ethan is glued to his video game console, and Emma … well, Emma is busy being Emma. Our relationship has been better, to say the least."

Jenna watched her sister's lip pulled to the side. She recognized the expression—she'd made it in the mirror hundreds of time worrying over Darren. "I guess I'm not the only one who's lonely."

"She's growing up and I just have to get used it. Soon she'll be going off to college. I need to find a new hobby."

"Baking is your hobby. Your pastries are to die for." Jenna bit into one of Sarah's blondies. Sugary sweetness and nostalgia filled her mouth.

"And I have two people to eat them." Sarah raised her left hand, waving her index and middle fingers in the air. "Mike and Dad. Keeps me busy, let me tell you."

"How about yoga?" Jenna didn't do yoga but knew plenty of women who did, and they all insisted it was the most relaxing thing ever—which was precisely why Jenna didn't do it. She needed her energy, flourished on stress. "Yoga is fun and relaxing, or so I've heard."

Her sister slow-blinked over the edge of her teacup. "I have no interest in twisting my body into a pretzel, thank you very much."

Well, at least they had that in common. "I'm sure you'll come up with something," Jenna encouraged her sister. "You always do."

Sarah cleared her throat. "So, how did it go with the contractor this morning? He's cute."

Jenna nearly choked on her blondie. She refused to let her thoughts settle for one second on Ben Fletcher's dimples. His perfect five o'clock scruff.

His toolbelt.

Jenna shoved another bite of blondie into her mouth. Swallowed. "He's *difficult!*"

"What do you mean?"

What did she mean? "He's annoyingly passionate about restoring the original beauty of the house and helping her rise up on her strong foundation again."

"Her?" Sarah wrinkled her nose. "Aunt May?"

"Apparently, the house is a *she.*"

Sarah groaned into her tea, picking up on Jenna's vibe. "Is he completely crazy? This is a renovation project, not a makeover."

"He's not crazy," Jenna corrected. "He's a control freak. He wants to do everything his way."

"But it's *our* house!"

Jenna hit her chest with her palm. "That's what I said! It's not like we're fixing the house up to move in. We're just trying to fulfill

Aunt May's wishes so we can all move on. But Ben thinks *she* deserves better."

Sarah narrowed her eyes, but Jenna wasn't sure if her sister's glare was directed at her or Ben Fletcher.

"Did you fire him?"

Jenna bit her lip and set the blondie back on the tray. "He kind of ... quit."

"He *quit*?"

"He was only interested in doing things his way, and not listening to me at all." Jenna squared her shoulders. Sure, maybe he'd had a couple of good ideas, but Ben had acted like it was his house—his budget—and hadn't seemed to hear her at all. Just like Darren, and just like Orville Barrington.

Sarah's face fell. "So, what are we going to do now?"

"I don't know." Jenna sighed. Frankly, she'd been wondering the same thing all evening. Had she made the right call in being so adamant about time and savings? Aunt May had chosen Ben for a reason. Perhaps she should have been more willing to hear his ideas. Then again, she had a life to get back to, even if it was smaller now than it had been a week ago. "But I just want to hire someone to get the job done, and get it done fast, so we can sell the house and I can get on with my life."

Without Aunt May to talk to, there was only one other person Jenna could trust for advice. "Is Dad around?"

"He's out in his workshop." Sarah's voice was flat. "Maybe he'll have some ideas."

Chapter Twelve

The approaching Hawaiian sunset painted the sky in brushstrokes of brilliant pinks and golds, but the colors over her head did nothing to brighten Jenna's mood as she made her way to the workshop behind Sarah's house. Jim Burke's RV was parked at the edge of her sister's property. Makeshift living quarters. Jenna's smile felt sad. She'd known Aunt May had aged, but when had her father gotten so old? Moving into Sarah's had seemed like a convenience at the time, but as Jenna took in the old surfboards and faded family photographs tacked along his workspace walls, she realized the change had been much more significant. While she had been so caught up in moving forward, time had passed her by.

"Can I talk to you a minute, Dad?"

Jim glanced up from his position on the floor where he was working with a handheld sander to smooth out the legs of what might one day be a small table. "As many minutes as you need, Peanut."

Jenna studied the large piece of wood, the shaping legs. "What are you working on?"

"Coffee table for May. Well, at least it was supposed to be. Was supposed to be for her room at the retirement home. Kou wood from one of her favorite trees on her property."

Kou wood. Jenna remembered the kou trees she had added into Terrace Pines. Funny, she'd meant them to bring a little bit of the islands home to her model. Instead, she'd found herself brought home to the islands.

"It's beautiful," Jenna said. "I'm sure the family would love to have a piece of her home to keep after we sell it."

Her father turned his attention back to the in-progress coffee table. He laid a heavy hand on the wood. "Maybe so."

"That is, *if* we can sell it." Tension tickled along the edges of Jenna's skin and she crossed her arms, so she didn't fidget. Telling Sarah about her bad day with Ben had been hard. Telling her father was way worse.

"What do you mean?"

Jenna tightened her grip on herself. "I wasn't seeing eye-to-eye with the contractor on how to reno the house, so he quit."

Her father blinked up in surprise. "Get out of here. Ben Fletcher didn't quit—boy doesn't know how."

It was Jenna's turn to be surprised. "Wait, how did you know who the contractor was?"

"Oh, Ben's been doing work for May for years." Jim waved her away. "He might be the only one left besides the two of us who loves her house as much as we do. Can't believe he'd quit on you, Peanut."

"Well, he did, Dad." *Sort of.*

Jim Burke didn't look convinced. If anything, he looked confused. "Just doesn't sound like Ben is all."

Jenna resisted the urge to groan. How come it didn't matter how old she got, she never grew out of worrying about disappointing her dad? Then again, it wasn't like she'd fired Ben. *He'd* walked out on *her.* Jenna nodded, widened her eyes, and prepared to insist on the point. Then, she reconsidered.

"Okay, I might have pushed him a little," she admitted. She dug the toe of her shoe into the dirt floor of the workshop. "A lot."

Jim gave her a fatherly look. "Doesn't sound like you either, Peanut."

She shrugged.

"Well, I'm sorry to hear he quit. May wanted him for this job every bit as much as she wanted you. We'll have to ask Grace if the will's flexible enough to let us find somebody new."

"That's only half the problem," Jenna said. "This is starting to look like it's going to take a long time—too long. May's house is in bad shape, Dad. Really bad. And I need to get home."

"Home," Jim repeated. His stoic expression cracked into something like hurt. "I've always thought of this as your home, Jenna. Doesn't matter if you live somewhere else ... Hawaii will always be your home."

"Maybe so, but I have to go back. Even if Maui is home, my life is in LA."

What's left of it anyway, she thought. She watched as her dad swapped out the sander for a large sheet of sandpaper and began rubbing away at the table legs. Hard.

"I still think you should finish the house," she said. "Then live there yourself."

He lifted his hand and pointed to his RV, at the surfboard leaned against its side. "And give up my luxurious lifestyle in Betty Lou here? No chance." He laughed. "I love being able to drive my house to my secret surf spots. When those big swells come in, it's just me, my board, and those waves."

This made Jenna smile. Her daddy might have gotten older, but he was still the same man who'd raised her—all sunshine and saltwater. "My surf rat Daddy."

Jim winked. "Besides, May didn't leave the house to me. She left it to you and Sarah to decide what to do … and I know Sarah once dreamed of opening up her own bakery when she was a girl. She doesn't say much about it, maybe doesn't even remember it herself, but I do."

A bakery? The thought of her sister making a business out of her baked goods made perfect sense. "She's never mentioned a bakery to me."

"Emma's almost grown and Ethan's not far behind. When those kids leave the nest, she'll need a new purpose in life. Already does, but she's still too busy grieving what she's lost than thinking about what's to come. She'll get there. So will you."

Jenna wasn't so sure about herself, but even without kids, she could still understand her sister's predicament. After all, she'd recently come very close to ending up with his and hers home offices.

The two sat together quietly for a few moments, the only sound the noise of Jim's sandpaper working against the bulk of kou tree. "Well, I guess I better go figure out what my options are. Either way it goes, May's house isn't going to renovate itself."

She gave her father a hug, then walked back to the house. Sunset had darkened into twilight, but though the sky was darker somehow Jenna's mood seemed just a fraction brighter.

❧

Sarah's small guest bedroom was nearly as big as Jenna's entire apartment. She plopped on the bed, opened her laptop, and stared at the familiar picture on her screen.

"I miss you, Aunt May." One more glance and Jenna blinked away tears and queued up her inbox. It had only been two days since she'd left the office, but she hadn't had a chance to check in and her email inbox was already overflowing. The sender's name at the top of her inbox made her stomach churn.

"Ugh, leave me alone Darren." She hit the delete key and discovered she could breathe easier without her ex-boyfriend's unread email at the top of her mailbox.

Most of the remaining emails were from Patti. Jenna sighed and glanced at the clock on the bedside table. Seven p.m. Patti would probably still be in the office. Maybe a quick call would be more productive than a dozen email responses.

Jenna pulled her cell from her pocket and looked at the screen. "Give me some bars, Maui!" she groaned. Reason ninety-nine why she needed to be back in LA—reliable cell service. Not only did the island run on its own clock, it had its own opinion about cellular communications as well. Wi-Fi was a whole different can of worms. She could barely refresh her social media much less download anything with any degree of reliability. Each time she'd tried to refresh her inbox, the entire app had crashed.

Surely Sarah had free long-distance calling, right? The island might run on its own time, but certainly it had made its way into modern phone service plans. Jenna tossed her cell phone on the bed, picked up the landline, and dialed Patti's office number.

Patti picked up on the second ring. "Patti Murray."

"Hey boss."

"Jenna! I was hoping you'd call. How are you doing?"

Jenna could hear the sound of Patti's nails clicking away against her keyboard in the background as the line transitioned to speaker phone. "I'm okay... No, I'm not okay, but I will be."

"I know you will be," Patti clipped back. "Look, I'm in the office working late, so please tell me you're on the beach with a Mai-Tai in one hand and a handsome surfer in the other."

Right. First of all, Patti always worked late. Second, the last thing Jenna had time for was a fruity cocktail or a cute guy. An image of Ben flashed through her thoughts—blue eyes, blond hair, tan skin—and she rolled her eyes. "Not hardly. Actually, there are some complications with Aunt May's estate. It's why I'm calling. I'm going to need more time on the ground here."

More time. What an understatement. Hopefully Patti wouldn't ask for anything more concrete, like a date on the calendar. Jenna couldn't stand the thought of disappointing yet another person today with bad news.

Patti's fingernails kept tapping. "Take all the time you need. We're fine."

"But my inbox—" She didn't bother to clarify she couldn't possibly keep up with her email anyway, not with its lag and island Wi-Fi.

"Don't worry about your inbox. It's mostly FYI." There was a momentary pause. "By the way, Darren keeps popping his head in my office, hoping I've heard from you."

Jenna's eyes rolled so hard she nearly gave herself a migraine. "Seems like he's willing to put more effort into talking to me *after* we've broken up than while we were together."

She could hear Patti's grin. "There's the Jenna Burke I've missed."

Her boss's fingernails resume their keyboard clacking. "Thanks, Patti."

"Think of me when you're on the beach."

Sure. Jenna laughed and hung up.

A ding on her laptop signaled another incoming message as her inbox queue finally caught up. Still thinking of Darren's newfound interest in communication, Jenna had her finger poised above the delete button before she saw the name of the sender. She froze.

May Burke.

"What. Is. Happening?"

Jenna clicked to open the email, but no luck. She gritted her teeth and clicked again. In a counterattack, her cursor devolved into a pinwheel. Again.

"Don't you spinning pinwheel of death me!" she growled.

She clicked again and her screen froze, even the pinwheel stopped moving. Jenna slammed her laptop closed. Well, her aunt's message was a surprise, and Jenna had no clue whether it was a good one. Based on what she'd seen in movies, messages received from beyond the grave usually weren't. What in the world might Aunt May be trying to communicate to her—and why now?

Chapter Thirteen

Aunt May's funeral service was small and intimate, every bit as warm and inviting as the woman herself had been. Jenna was surprised at the number of people who turned up—most were friends and family, but there were many others, unfamiliar faces she didn't recognize who'd known and loved Aunt May too. Just like at her memorial. It was no surprise the woman had left her mark on so many people, but Jenna couldn't help but wonder if she'd left anyone else any special surprises in her will or if the pleasure had been reserved just for Sarah and her.

Well, and Ben Fletcher too, she supposed.

When the service was over, a few friends and relatives lingered to share their condolences with the family. Jenna stood beside her sister and father, accepting hugs, handshakes, and sympathy cards as the well-wishers shuffled past. Still in New York, Grace had sent a lovely spray of lilies and ivy. Her note had smugly suggested Jenna plant the ivy at Aunt May's.

Ben had observed the service from the back pew of the chapel. Jenna had given him a polite smile when they'd made eye contact, but otherwise she'd refused to notice how nice he cleaned up in a trim black suit which had shown off his broad shoulders and narrow hips. He'd given her a small nod when he passed through the line to shake hands with her father, but had slipped through the doors after the service without saying anything. Fine by her.

When everyone else had gone and the chapel empty, Jenna moved forward for her turn with Aunt May. She wanted a few minutes to herself to say goodbye to the woman who had stepped in after her mother had passed away and finished raising her. The finality of the moment caught in Jenna's throat. This was truly goodbye.

"I'll be just a second." Jenna touched her sister's arm as Sarah, Mike, and the kids turned to make their way out of the chapel and toward a future without Aunt May.

Sarah nodded. She dabbed at the tears in the corner of her eye with a handkerchief, and allowed herself to be led away by her husband.

"I'll stay, too," Jim said.

He looked to Jenna for approval and she nodded. Alone sounded better with two. Together, Jenna and her father moved to stand beside Aunt May's casket. Jim hadn't said a word throughout the service. How heavy was the weight of things unsaid? Jenna supposed it must be quite a lot.

After a few moments of quiet, Jim draped his arm over Jenna's shoulders and gave her a gentle squeeze. He sniffed. "My sister was a heck of a gal, wasn't she, Peanut?"

"She was." She leaned into her dad's embrace, grateful for the comfort. "There were so many people here I didn't know. It shows how much people loved her. And it was so nice to hear their stories. They brought back so many wonderful memories."

"Those are the best parts of her to live on. Remember the old tire swing on the big oak tree in her yard?"

Jenna laughed as memories of her swinging on the tire swing—and her dad untangling the rope numerous times after she'd worn it out—came back to her. "I put a lot of miles on that swing."

"May's idea. I told her you wouldn't use it, but she knew better. She spent hours trying to throw that rope over the highest, sturdiest limb." Jim sniffed again, happy memories breaking through his sadness as he pulled his arm away and rubbed his hands. "And her strawberry field? Do you remember? I imagine it's nothing but dust and dried-up roots by now."

"Oh, I loved her fresh strawberries!" Jenna remembered plucking the sweet fruits from the vine, gathering basketfuls her mom and Sarah would use to make fresh pies and jams. Had she seen the patch when she'd been at the house? So little remained of her aunt's once-beautiful gardens it was hard to be sure.

"She was allergic to them." Jim laughed, all traces of tears gone from his voice now. "She tended that garden for years wearing rubber gloves. She did it for you and Sarah."

"You can't be serious!" A flashback of Aunt May plucking strawberries in rubber gloves flashed into Jenna's memory. At the time she'd assumed it was some gardener's quirk she was too young to appreciate. Now it made more sense. "Come to think of it, I remember her tending the gardens, but never saw her eat a strawberry. Guess now I know why." She made a mental note to replant the strawberries, right after she tucked Grace's ivy into the soil.

"The Easter egg hunts, the luaus, and the holiday sleepovers," her dad reflected, each remembrance bringing fresh memories to the forefront of Jenna's thoughts.

"She really knew how to celebrate the seasons," Jenna agreed, now thinking about how Aunt May's house had looked all decked out for Christmas. She'd worked with her aunt to trace each eave of the large Victorian in white mini lights. They'd wrapped yards of green garland around every column and palm in the front lawn. Decked every door and window with a wreath so the house seemed alive with yuletide cheer. "When Sarah and I were kids, we'd watch scary movies together. Aunt May would let us stay up past midnight."

Jim nodded. "You girls had your own room there for years. Sometimes I worried you two would never come back home, you were so comfortable. At home."

Home. Jenna gave her dad a squeeze. "Of course we would, but Aunt May's was definitely home away from home. Bunk beds and sugary cereal—who could resist?"

"She was an excellent second mother to you girls. You two were the daughters she always wished she had. She lived for you and Sarah."

"She really did, didn't she?"

She's still here, Jenna thought. May had left them the house, the renovation. She remembered the surprise email in her inbox last night, still waiting, unread. Aunt May was gone, but apparently not finished.

Jim opened his arms to Jenna, and she moved into them, giving her dad a bigger hug than she'd given anyone in a long time. "Come on, let's go home," he said as they pulled away from the embrace. "I bet Sarah has cooked up something extra special for such a sad day."

"It's not that sad, Dad," Jenna asserted. She reconsidered. "Well, of course it's sad, but remembering all these wonderful memories makes it hard to stay sad."

Jim nodded. "You're right. All those old memories, all the old joy and happiness, that's what May always wanted to leave behind.

Just like her house."

Jenna's eyebrows twisted. There was something important in her father's words, but she couldn't put her finger on it. "What do you mean?"

"My sister had a funny thing about making sure whatever she left behind was worth holding on to. Not just memories—those fade. May wanted a part of her to live on. To leave its mark. To keep her spirit alive. That's why she left the house to you and your sister—and why she picked Ben to help you with the renovation."

"I think Aunt May might have misjudged that one a little," Jenna grumped. "I think he's a little nuts. He refers to May's house as a *she*."

"Kind of like I do with Betty Lou?"

Her father had a point. She shrugged.

"Ben spent a lot of time with your aunt over the years, even after she went into the home. Always helped out where he could, though I don't think she ever paid him one red cent. When her condition got bad enough she started thinking about her estate, well, Ben was the one she called. She wanted to fix it up, sell it off so it didn't weigh the family down. Ben refused. He told her the house was her legacy, that he wanted her family and the world to have something to remember her by a hundred years from now." Jim laughed. "Right up May's alley."

Jenna thought of the name painted on the side of Ben's work truck. *Legacy Renovations*. Of course.

The past week had hit Jenna like a wrecking ball. First losing the pitch to Barrington, then getting dumped by Darren—both had left cracks at the very foundation of everything she'd worked so hard for: a rising career and a marriage to the perfect partner. Aunt May's passing had been the last swing of a very destructive hammer, shattering Jenna's already fragile heart into a million pieces of grief and doubt and failure.

The surprise of inheriting her aunt's dilapidated home—and being saddled with the task of renovating it—had twisted her grief into frustration. In all her preoccupation with the things she'd lost, Jenna had failed to appreciate the gift May had given her. Renovating the home wasn't an obligation or a waste of her time, even if she wasn't planning on living in the house. It was an opportunity, a blessing disguised as a chore. Aunt May had given the niece who'd loved building the chance to rebuild something from nothing, to imbue her own vision into the house she had loved as much as her aunt had. Even Sarah, who'd never been one for building things, loved putting together things from scratch, and Aunt May had thought of that too. Nails and tiling were ingredients in the recipe for a beautiful home.

As Jenna walked arm in arm with her dad to the parking lot, her gaze fell on a dirty gray truck. Halfway across the parking lot, with his suit jacket off and the sleeves of his dress shirt rolled up, Ben leaned against his truck.

Had he waited for her? No, of course not—why would he? Regardless, Jenna knew an opportunity when she saw one.

"Wish me luck, Dad," Jenna said. She gave her father a quick kiss on the cheek then, without giving herself time to second guess her next move, she took off in the direction of the pickup, waving her arms to get Ben's attention. "Ben, wait!"

Surprise was evident on Ben's face. He opened the truck's door, but didn't climb in. Instead, he leaned against the cab and waited as she rushed toward him.

"I need to apologize," Jenna started when she reached the truck. She held her finger up and paused, catching her breath from her short run under the warm summer sun. "You were right. I was wrong. Aunt May's legacy deserves better than the basic renovations I wanted to do, and so does her house. Will you reconsider the job?"

When he didn't answer, she added, "Please?"

Ben chewed on his response for longer than Jenna thought entirely polite, but eventually his posture softened.

"For your aunt, I will. But here are my conditions." He caught Jenna's exasperated sigh and gave her a stern look. "No laminate. Fireplace stays. We knock down a wall to open up the floor plan. Both bathrooms and the kitchen are complete remodels, preserving as much of the original plumbing hardware as possible."

"*Maybe* no laminate," Jenna countered. "We do still have a budget to work within, and I'm responsible for ensuring May's money covers the renovation."

Ben narrowed his eyes, but eventually acquiesced. "We can *revisit* the flooring together. But definitely new crown molding, ceiling fans, and low VOC paint."

Okay, this wasn't bad. Jenna nodded her approval at Ben's list, stalling only on the last. "What's VOC paint?"

"Volatile organic compound. You know that really potent new-paint smell?"

She nodded.

"Low VOC reduces it. Also reduces the carbon footprint. Unstable chemicals in high VOC paints let off harmful gases toxic to people and the environment."

"Oh," Jenna breathed, simultaneously impressed by Ben's attention to environmentally friendly construction details and tucking that bit of knowledge away for future use. If she ever got her chance to build the sustainable architectures she dreamed of, low VOC paint was something she wanted to be sure she specified in her estimate. "Yes, of course that's fine."

"*And...*" Ben smirked, not finished with his list of requirements. "A new back porch. No steps."

"Fine." Remembering May's strawberries, Jenna added a condition of her own. "But not too big. Aunt May used to have a garden in the back. I want to revive it and will need the space."

Ben stuck out a hand and Jenna slipped her palm into his before he could change his mind.

"The house is always right?" he asked.

Jenna understood. They'd work together to do what was best for the house, putting aside their differences for the good of the cause—and Aunt May's legacy.

"The house is always right," she confirmed.

"Deal. When do we start?"

"Monday."

Nodding, Ben opened the pickup's driver's side door and stepped one leg in. "I'll see you then. Bring your hammer."

Jenna flinched. "I architect and design. I don't provide free labor."

"Whatever you say. But we'll get things done twice as fast if there were two of us."

Two? "Don't you have employees?"

"I'm a one-man crew." Ben gave Jenna another one of those mischievous looks he'd shown when they'd inspected the house together. "May told me you were pretty good with tools. She used to brag about you all the time."

It was Jenna's turn to smirk. "I haven't so much as held a hammer in years. I'm not sure I could tell the different between a Phillips-head and a flathead screwdriver anymore."

Ben settled himself inside the cab of his truck and shut the door. "The flathead is the one with the flat head," he quipped through the open window.

Jenna rolled her eyes. "It was a figure of speech."

"Not a very good one." Ben cranked the truck engine to life. "Besides, it'll come back to you. Like riding a bike."

"No, it won't," Jenna called as Ben's truck began to inch away. "Because I don't ride bikes!"

"If you say so." Ben waved out the open window and sped away.

Was he referring to Jenna's assertion she wouldn't be joining him at Aunt May's or about her resistance to bike riding? It didn't matter either way so long as he took the job, which—Jenna smiled to herself—he had.

Chapter Fourteen

At dusk, Jenna traded her prim funeral attire for an old pair of jeans and a tank top, and headed out into the workshop to give her father a hand. She stood at the edge of the workshop for a moment, watching Jim sand the kou tree turned coffee table. The piece was beginning to take shape. A few minutes later, he turned off the sander and sat back, then pulled a carpenter pencil from the old canvas apron he always wore when woodworking and chewed at the tip.

"Hey, Dad."

"Peanut!" Jim exclaimed, looking up from his work. "What are you doing here?"

Jenna ran her hand over the smooth surface of the kou. Pinched the fine layer of sawdust between her thumb and forefinger. "Don't sound so happy to see me," she joked, snatching up a cloth to clear away the grit. "I'm just here to help."

Her father's face crinkled around the edges in a grin. "Do you remember how to use tools?"

"Someone recently told me it's like riding a bike."

Jim laughed, but the sound was warm. "And when was the last time *you* rode a bike?"

"About twenty years ago."

Jim laughed again, then tucked the pencil into one of the

pockets of his apron. He snapped his fingers. "I have something for you," he said, stepping away to the back of the large workspace. He climbed up on a footstool and retrieved something made of black and brown leather, then stepped back down, extending the item to her as he unfolded it.

"Are you serious?" Jenna recognized the toolbelt in her dad's hands and her heart skipped. "I haven't seen this in forever."

"It was torn," Jim explained. "I had it sewn back up and the leather cleaned, metal shined. Always hoped you might have use for it again someday."

Jenna secured the toolbelt around her waist and ran her hands over the tools she'd treasured so much when she'd been a young girl. Her fingers landed on her favorite of all the items in her belt and she pulled out the hammer, then held it up to the dim light of deepening twilight so she could inspect the ivory handle and black rubber grip. Below the metal head was a ring of imitation rubies, sparkling red in the light. "Ruby. Oh my gosh, I had no idea you still had her."

"She's been here all this time. I polished her up for you and replaced the missing gemstones." Her dad beamed. He handed her a nail and watched as she hammered it deftly into a piece of spare wood. "Looks like it is like riding a bike after all."

Jenna found it hard to disagree. Having Ruby in her hand again felt amazing.

"So, are you going to get some use out of her? It would be nice to have you around for a while, Peanut. I know May would be happy to see you back out working on her house. Well, guess it's *your* house now."

"Only for a little while," Jenna clarified, not wanting her dad to get too attached to the idea of her visit to the island becoming permanent. "But Ben did agree to come back to work on the house, and my boss did tell me to take all the time I need. I might as well get in on the action while I'm here."

"Patti Murray is a smart lady," Jim agreed. "Almost as smart as your dear old dad."

She spun the hammer in her hands and holstered it in her toolbelt just like she'd done as a girl. Suddenly, she couldn't wait to get back to Aunt May's and get her hands dirty.

❧

Jenna was already at Aunt May's the next morning when Ben pulled up in his pickup. She watched over the curled edges of her faded blueprint as he slid from his truck and came toward her, a sledgehammer clutched in each hand.

He grinned at her as he made his way up the front steps. "You beat me to work. And you have a blueprint?"

"Just wanted to show you that mainlanders can also be punctual." She pointed at the paper. "And my dad never throws anything away."

"Huh." Ben's eyes swept over her from ponytail to blue jeans, lingering a moment too long on the toolbelt around her waist. "There's nothing quite like a woman with a toolbelt," he noted with a sheepish smile. He peered down at Ruby, glinting red in the fresh morning sunlight, and his smile grew into a smirk, causing his dimples to deepen and Jenna's heart to flutter. "That's a pretty hammer you've got, but you're going to need something a little more powerful today—it's demo day."

He handed her one of the sledgehammers and the weight of it took Jenna by surprise. The hammer slipped in her grasp. Its head nearly crashed through one of the rotten planks of the porch, but she managed to keep the thing from slamming headfirst into more damage they'd have to fix. Barely.

She steadied the top-heavy instrument against her shoulder and tried to look confident. Talking about opening up the house's floor plan had felt a lot more reasonable before she was the one wielding a blunt object. "Tell me again why we're demolishing walls?"

"Because old homes like this were built with lots of small rooms separated by walls that prevent natural light from entering," Ben replied, repeating words Jenna herself had said only a few days earlier. "We have to open up space to create views in the rear of the house and increase the amount of sunlight running through."

Again, it *sounded* reasonable, but the weight currently bruising Jenna's shoulder insisted otherwise. She groaned. "I can barely hold this thing up."

"That's because you haven't found your motivation yet."

"What does that mean?" Jenna rolled her eyes. Had she really already forgotten just how smug Ben Fletcher could be?

"Demo day is the perfect time to blow off some steam, but you obviously lead a perfect life," Ben goaded. "The perfect job in the city, the successful boyfriend who wears a suit to work every day. An aunt who leaves you a big house with the costs covered ..." He let his words linger, dimples deepening as he grinned at her, seeming to enjoy ruffling her feathers. "Demolition day is not for someone with a charmed life. Maybe I pegged you all wrong, *Peanut*."

He turned to walk through the front door just as the heat brewing inside Jenna's chest bubbled over and came spilling out of her mouth. "Stop right there!" she demanded. "Just who do you—"

But Ben had already slipped through the door, sending Jenna's temper flaring in his wake. Left gasping at the audacity, Jenna staggered through the threshold after him, lugging the stupidly heavy sledgehammer with her. Funny, it didn't seem so heavy now—a realization which only infuriated her more.

"You don't know the first thing about me!" Jenna was ready to unleash fire when she caught up with Ben in the living room. "I loved my aunt, but I didn't ask for this house. And I would give it up in a second to have her back. On top of that, my boyfriend—whom I dated for *four* years—broke up with me literally the day Aunt May died, so he's not so perfect after all. And my career is not nearly as fulfilling as I thought it would be. I lost my biggest deal ever over five percent!"

"Don't tell me, Toolbelt," Ben yawned. "Take it out on the wall."

Jenna's jaw dropped. *Toolbelt?* Ben Fletcher was the *last* person on earth who was going to give her a nickname. Who did this guy think he was, anyway? A building contractor moonlighting as a psychotherapist? She'd put the sledgehammer straight through his face!

Frustrated and fueled by adrenaline, Jenna hoisted the heavy hammer and slammed it through the wall.

A large piece of sheetrock crashed to the floor and with it a sense of calm flooded out Jenna's ire.

"That felt good," she breathed. "If I'd known breaking things could be so liberating, I'd have started slamming holes in walls a long time ago."

"It was a good swing, too," Ben noted appreciatively. "Except that's the wrong wall. That one's staying."

Jenna gawked in newfound horror at the very expensive

therapy session she'd just enjoyed. The hole in the wall was bigger than a basketball. "What?!"

"Just kidding."

She picked up the hammer and swung again.

Chapter Fifteen

T he afternoon passed in a blur of drywall dust and broken plaster.

Ben and Jenna took up a tempo as they slammed sledgehammers into plaster. With one hammering first and then the other, the sound of their twin beats made a quick two-step as they worked side by side, opening up the floor plan and inviting more natural light to spread throughout the newly expanded rooms. The house had been dark and boxy before, but Aunt May had employed lamps to give the house its cozy glow. Now, real sunlight filtered through, bringing warmth with it.

At first, Jenna found the sledgehammer heavy and awkward, but she focused every bit of energy she had on each swing. By the time they'd gotten halfway through the first wall, the tool felt like a natural extension of her arm—long, muscular, and powerful, as if she'd used it a hundred times before. With every lift and fall, she felt more invigorated and more resolute, as if she were breaking up more than pieces of old drywall. Like she was breaking something open within herself.

Jenna swung and *crack* went her frustrations about Terrace Pines. Another whack and *smash*, the part of her still holding onto the uncomfortable shame she'd clung to over her doomed relationship with Darren fell away. When a particular piece of the wall stubbornly stuck in a stud, she dropped the sledgehammer and used her body as a mallet, pummeling the piece with her foot until it crumbled, taking every bit of insecurity Jenna had with it until she felt like she'd been stuck in a plaster shell of herself and only now had broken free. Even Ben seemed to appreciate her determination … and pity the wall.

When they'd finished hammering down one wall, Ben and Jenna hauled chunks of broken drywall to a dumpster out front. They took down another wall after lunch. The second was easier than the first, and Jenna found herself having fun. It became a game: Ben hit first and then she swung, the two counting points between them to see who dislodged the most pieces.

Afterward, Jenna sat in one of the rockers on the back porch, rehydrating with a large glass of water from the jugs they'd brought in until the plumbing could be fixed. Ben walked out and sat in the chair next to her, stretching out his long legs in front of him like a cat basking in the summer sun.

He rolled his head to the side to look at her. "I wouldn't want to be a sheetrock wall with you staring down at me, sledgehammer in hand."

"Neither would I," Jenna agreed. "That felt good. Better than good, actually."

Ben laughed, stretching again, and took a swig from the thermos he'd carried out onto the porch with him. "Demo day is my favorite day of a reno. I may not be a rich man, so days on the yacht are out of the picture, but most people don't get to bust down walls every day. Simple pleasures are more fun. Don't you think?"

Jenna, who had been on a yacht, thought beating down a wall was infinitely more entertaining than sitting on a stuffy boat. She'd never liked the water anyway—a dark secret she'd harbored during a childhood spent growing up on an island. "It was fun."

"I'm glad you agree, because there's a lot more fun to be had." Ben looked over his shoulder at the house, squinting as he peered in through the dusty windows at the rooms beyond. "A *lot* more."

It might have sounded ominous coming from anybody else, but from Ben it sounded anticipatory, almost eager. Jenna pulled her knees up to her chest and hugged them against her, resting her head on her forearm to gaze at the man beside her. "You really love what you do, don't you?"

One side of Ben's mouth lifted upward in a smirk, making the dimple in his profile wink at Jenna as his eyes swept over the backyard. "There's nothing like the feeling of breathing new life into an old house with a complete gut renovation. It goes from run down and unappreciated, to shiny and new and full of potential. It's a second act for the structure, gives it a chance to start new. Everyone and everything—even a broken-down old house— deserves a second act."

Jenna considered Ben's words. It was kind of poetic when you thought of it like that, which she hadn't ... until now. "And your second act? What's it going to be?"

"You're looking at it." Ben laughed and took another swig from his thermos. "After college, I moved to the city and worked in sales. Man, nothing can break a man's spirit like working in sales. I needed a full reno myself by the time I got out here."

"Sales?" Jenna repeated, surprise creeping into her voice. "What kind of sales?"

"Advertising." He spat the word out like it tasted bitter.

Jenna almost giggled, thinking of the strapping contractor all buttoned up and wearing a Bluetooth in his ear rather than a toolbelt around his waist. "I would never have guessed."

"Why not? Don't think I'm persuasive enough?"

Jenna had to laugh. "Oh, I *know* you are. You just don't seem like the salesman type."

Ben lifted his index finger. He pointed it at her as if she'd guessed his secret. "Turns out I'm not. In fact, it nearly drove me crazy. I wasn't good at sitting behind a desk. It took me three years to figure out why I was so miserable. Eventually, I wised up. Moved back home and started my own business."

"*Legacy Renovations*," Jenna filled in. "I like it. Now I see what the name means."

"So did your Aunt May. I gave her my 'second chances' talk, and she hired me on the spot."

Jenna smiled, but decided not to share what her father had told her. "I heard you two were close."

Closer than you let on, she thought. Ben nodded but averted his gaze. His eyes had gone a little misty.

"I miss our conversations, your aunt and me. We would talk about all sort of things classic—homes, movies, cars. May was a lot of fun to talk to."

Still hugging her knees, Jenna exhaled. She'd give a lot for just one more conversation with her aunt. It was kind of a funny thing, talking to someone you loved. No matter how many conversations you had—how many laughs and cries and inside jokes—there was always room for one more. Conversations were like possibilities: limitless and irreplaceable. Jenna tried not to think about what she might have said to Aunt May if she'd known their last conversation would be their *last*. Would she have told her she loved her? Thanked her for always being there? The truth was, she probably wouldn't have been able to say any of those things, but in the end it wouldn't have mattered. Aunt May had already known.

"She told me once I reminded her of a young, Hawaiian Anne Baxter."

Ben gave her an appraising stare, then nodded. "I can see that."

"I still have no idea who she is," Jenna admitted.

"*All About Eve.*"

Jenna scrunched her nose. "Eve who?"

"It's a movie. A classic. About a Broadway star who gets displaced by an ambitious fan."

"Anne Baxter is the star?" Jenna guessed.

Ben stifled a laugh. "No, Bette Davis played the star. Anne was the ambitious fan."

"Ambitious sounds like a negative in this context," Jenna decided, narrowing her eyes.

"She *was* the antagonist."

Jenna rolled her eyes, not wanting to dissect why this particular role had reminded Ben of her. An antagonistic ambitious fan sounded a little too Annie Wilkes for her taste. "So, you went to college?" she asked in an attempt to redirect the conversation.

For someone who didn't like the fast-paced sales game, Ben was awfully quick on the uptake. "Does that surprise you?"

"No," Jenna countered, although it had. He didn't seem uneducated or anything, he just didn't strike her as a white-collar kind of guy. *Like Darren.* Jenna shoved that thought back to Broadway too. "Just … what you do, renovating homes … you know what I mean."

Ben grinned at her. "Like I said, I tried the advertising world and it wasn't for me. But yeah, I went to college. Got a bachelor's degree. Didn't help me much in advertising, but I'll admit it's come in handy a time or two as a sole proprietor." He looked at her out of the corner of his eye. "I just wanted to see you squirm."

"Thanks a lot."

"There's no home renovation college, is there? There should be. A lot to learn. Carpentry, plumbing, electrical. Even the cosmetic stuff, like spackling and laying grout. It all seems like it doesn't go together, but it does."

Jenna nodded in agreement. She was quickly learning that even studying architecture hadn't prepared her with all the necessary knowledge she needed. Sure, she could *design* a building—she knew the angles and construction theory and had a basic grasp on construction methods. But, as she'd discovered in the short amount of time she'd spent with Ben, she barely knew anything about the nitty-gritty details, like polyvinyl chloride flooring and low VOC paint. She hadn't even been totally confident on the difference between drywall and plaster until this morning, and this was only day one. Like Ben said, there was still a lot of fun to be had. *And a lot of learning too,* she supposed.

"So, you studied business in college, then?" she asked.

"Not really."

"What then?"

"Seventeenth-century Eastern European romantic literature."

For half a second, Jenna thought he was pulling her leg, then she burst out laughing.

"What?" he exclaimed, feigning offense. "What's so funny?"

"Nothing," she managed to choke out between giggles. "Just explains all the fancy language, that's all."

"Well…" Ben grinned. "I guess I'm a poet and didn't know it, Toolbelt."

This time, Jenna let the nickname slide.

Chapter Sixteen

By the time Jenna dragged herself back to her sister's house at the end of the day, everything on her body hurt. She slumped into a chair at Sarah's kitchen table and tried to remember what it felt like to have bones.

Sarah gave her a once over. "So, you look good," she teased.

"Oh, I'm sure I look like I just came in off the runway." Jenna rolled her eyes. Even the small motion hurt. She winced. How sore did one have to be for their facial muscles to hurt? "We got all the main demo done today. Sledgehammers."

"I don't know what that means, but I'm happy for you."

Jenna was too exhausted to explain, and the details probably wouldn't interest her sister anyway. She shifted in her seat and a muscle twanged in her back, the movement sending sparks shooting up her spine to erupt somewhere near the back of her ears. "Oh, my aching…" She sighed. "Everything, honestly. I need a long, hot soak in the tub. Please tell me you have Epsom salts?"

"I do." Sarah smiled. "I also have something else. Something you may like even more than Epsom salt."

What would feel better on her sore muscles than a warm hug from soaking salts? "A personal masseuse?"

"Better." Sarah pulled a tray of fresh brownies from her oven, then set them on a stone trivet on the table and pulled a pitcher of milk from the fridge. "*Bon appetit.*"

Jenna's mouth watered. "Seriously, you made *more* brownies?" Spurred forth by a sudden burst of energy, she leaned forward and plucked a pastry from the pan. She blew the brownie a couple times to make sure it was cool enough not to burn her tongue, then took a bite. Gooey, fudgy chocolate coated her tongue. The taste was nearly enough to make her moan—the tension melted from her muscles, all attention now focused on the taste in her mouth. "Maybe I'll skip the bath and just eat this whole tray."

Sarah preened as she wiped her hands on her apron. "Go for it. You'll work off the calories, and I can always bake more tomorrow."

Jenna recognized a familiar note in Sarah's voice. Disappointment sprinkled with failure and broken dreams. She'd sounded the same when she'd found out Barrington had walked. Another bite of brownie, and an idea sparked in Jenna's mind. "Dad mentioned your idea of opening a bakery once upon a time. You never told me that."

Sarah waved the suggestion away and took a seat at the table. She carved a brownie out for herself. "Oh, it's nothing. Just, you know … dreaming about the *what ifs* a long time ago. I love making people happy with my baking. Once I thought it could be more than just the people who live in my house." A lonely, bitter laugh escaped through her lips. "Of course, that crowd is getting pretty thin these days. Mike's so busy with his CPA work, and in not too many years, Emma won't need me as much anymore—not that she does now. Ethan either. The kids are growing up, and I'm just not as important as I used to be."

Sarah reached out across the table and took her sister's hand. Squeezed. "They'll always need you. We always needed Aunt

May."

"Maybe."

"Definitely."

Jenna took another bite of brownie, rolled in the delicious flavor, and held the half-eaten morsel in the air. "Honestly, Sarah. I love the bakery idea. You could make these and all the other treasures you could conjure out of thin air. It's brilliant. It has to happen. And this renovation project is going to make it possible. The funds we get from selling the house will be more than enough for you to start your own bakery."

Sarah's lip twisted, but her tone was hopeful. "You really think so?"

"Absolutely."

For the first time that evening, her sister's smile reached her eyes. "I really miss having you here, sis."

Jenna smiled around the bit of brownie still in her mouth. She really missed being there, too.

※

After another hard morning of work, Jenna and Ben sat cross-legged outside on the worn wooden planks of Aunt May's newly constructed back porch, soaking up the afternoon sun and enjoying a picnic lunch of subs and chips Jenna had scooped up from the local deli.

"This is so nice." Jenna breathed, enjoying the feel of the sun beating down on her arms as she took the last bite of her sandwich and leaned back on her elbows. "Maybe your idea of putting up a new back porch wasn't so bad after all. I could get used to this."

"I'll take that as a compliment." Ben laughed. "Life is good when you can eat lunch like this every day." He held up his water bottle in mock salute. "To the good life."

"Sure, why not?" Jenna lifted her water and clinked its tip against Ben's. "*HipaHipa.*"

"Cheers."

They sipped to complete their toast. The cool water rushing down Jenna's throat felt like heaven.

Ben finished his sandwich in two bites and pulled some hardwood and tile sample books from where he'd stashed them beside the construction-dust-stained cooler their lunch had kept cool in while they worked. "So, I was thinking we'll want the hardwood to flow into the wall tile of the kitchen. How do you see it?"

Jenna had been thinking on the topic this morning and arrived at the same conclusion, though she still wasn't totally committed to the idea of forsaking refurbishing the broken planks. "Just what you said, actually. Whatever we do with the flooring, it should flow into the tile wall." Finished with her sandwich, she took the sample book from Ben and flipped through. A sample caught her eye and she paused. *Perfect.* "Since the countertop is gray quartz, let's go with this travertine blue back splash."

She pointed at another page of complementary tile choices. "And finish with dark cabinets to match the floor."

Ben gave an approving nod. "And stainless-steel appliances?"

"Of course." What else would she choose? White? Jenna shuddered at the thought.

"I love it. Your sense of design is very impressive, ma'am."

Jenna beamed. "Apparently there's more to you than demo, sir," she returned.

Both chuckled. Ben extended his arm and swept his half-empty water bottle in front of them, left to right so he covered the spread of land before them. "So, this is all yours. Aren't you lucky? It's what, three or four acres?"

"Five." Jenna let her gaze linger on the expanse of green before her. The land was largely overrun with weeds and brambles, and the edge of the dense Hawaiian jungle had crept closer than she remembered, but staring at it from under a blue sky with the sun's heat beating down on her skin, the property seemed even more beautiful now than it had before. There weren't green spaces like this in the city, even the ones that had been architected to do their best imitations. The blue and white of the beach crashing just in the distance didn't hurt, either. "When I was a girl, my dad would take me out into the jungle for nature walks. I could walk forever in those woods."

"We should do that, then," Ben decided as he wiped away the last crumbs of his sandwich from his fingers and laid back on the porch, hands clasped behind his head. "Add an afternoon stroll into one of our days. Be a nice way to cool down after some hard work"

"No, thanks," said Jenna, recoiling. As pretty as it was to look at, she also remembered bug bites and what it felt like to get a rash from mango tree sap. The fruit was delicious, but the tree itself was a wicked relative to poison ivy. As a girl, Jenna had endured more rashes than she could count even if she used all her fingers and her toes. "I'm not a walk-in-the-woods kind of girl anymore."

"We don't grow out of nature." Ben gave her a look like she'd just sprouted a second head.

"If you loved the jungle so much as a kid, why wouldn't you love it now? It hasn't changed. That's kind of nature's thing."

"Then I changed, I guess." Jenna shrugged, an awkward

motion from her position reclined on her elbows. "We all do. Eventually, I grew up, and somewhere along the way I grew out of being the kind of girl who tromps around in the woods."

Ben winced and rolled onto his side to face her. He propped himself up on his elbow, then leaned close as if he was about to tell her a secret. "Remind me never to do that," he teased. "Must be what happens when you move away to the big city and decide not to come back."

Jenna sighed. Really? He was really going to go there? She frowned at him and hoped it deterred his current train of thought.

It didn't. "Come on," he pressed. "I spilled my guts already about my failed career in ad sales, so it's your turn."

Fine. "All right. What do you want to know?"

Ben took a sip of water and shrugged. "How you go from an island girl to a big-time Los Angeles architect?"

Big time. Yeah right. "Not so big-time. I'm just a junior partner at my firm."

She looked at Ben, but he was still staring at the trees, so she rolled her eyes and continued. "Okay, fine. After high school, Dad tried his best to guide me, but frankly I was a little lost. Knocked around some odd jobs for a while, couldn't figure out what I really wanted to do with my life. Aunt May eventually kicked me out of the nest, advised me to do what I love and said the money would take care of itself. So, I decided to follow my angles and math my way into college."

"That's when you moved to LA."

Jenna nodded. "Patti hired me right out of college on the merits of my capstone alone. She said I had something special— lots of potential, that sort of thing. I've been at Avery Architects ever since. Like I said I'm just a junior partner right now, but occasionally—" She grinned. "In my dreams, I'm Frank Lloyd Wright. Maybe one day I'll even have my own firm."

Ben peered at her out of the corner of his eyes. "I'm afraid to say he and I haven't had the pleasure of meeting."

Jenna couldn't stop a laugh. "Well, probably a good thing, considering Frank Lloyd Wright passed away decades ago." When Ben continued to stare, she added, "Frank Lloyd Wright was an incredible architect, designer, and educator. He designed over one thousand buildings during his career, always designing to put humanity in harmony with the environment. He called it 'organic architecture.' It's the same priority I put into my work."

Ben smiled and tipped his water bottle against hers in another solute. "To Mr. Wright."

"To Anne Baxter."

Ben's eyes hung on Jenna's a little too long and he looked away, cleared his throat. "What do you love best about being an architect?" he asked.

This was an easy one. "The first look a client has when they walk into a finished job and you realize you've totally nailed it, fulfilled their hopes and dreams. They usually wipe away a few tears of happiness. I live for those tears, that happiness."

"Wow."

He sounded impressed, but Jenna's smile turned wistful as her thoughts wandered to Terrace Pines. "But I guess sometimes having your happiness depend on others' happiness is a risky proposition, right?"

"Maybe," Ben agreed. 'But isn't that what it's all about?"

"What what's all about?"

His eyes found hers, and again they hung on too long. This time, however, Ben didn't look away. "Love."

Jenna felt as if she were being tugged down, like the specks in Ben's gaze were magnets drawing her into him. She forgot about losing her pitch, or about all the reasons she'd left the island. Reasons she hadn't come back. Or whatever it was it was they had been talking about. All she thought about now was another dimple in his jaw she'd somehow missed before. Another shade of blue hiding in his eyes.

"Uh. I wasn't talking about love," she managed.

"Sure you were," Ben said. "My question was what do you love best about being an architect. And you told me. In life, in work, with people, love should be at the heart of everything we're about." He held her gaze for a heartbeat longer and then blinked, breaking the spell. Clearing his throat, Ben propelled himself back up to a sitting position and Jenna turned her attention elsewhere, anywhere that wasn't warm and deep and inviting—or specked with gold.

"We should get back to banging nails," he said, his voice uncharacteristically brusque.

A dreamy feeling had collected in the back of her throat, and Jenna swallowed it back. She was here to renovate Aunt May's house, not swap googly eyes with the ruggedly handsome contractor slash romantic literature bard.

"Back to work," she agreed.

Chapter Seventeen

Sarah had just finished unloading the dishwasher when her cell phone rang. She almost refused the call when she saw Unknown Number on the screen, but curiosity got the better of her and she decided to answer. It wasn't like she was busy doing much else anyway.

"This is Sarah Maxwell." She pursed her lips, impressed by how professional her own voice sounded.

On the other end of the line, a man cleared his throat. "Sarah, it's Darren. Darren Taylor."

Sarah moved her thumb automatically to end the call, but she hesitated. What on earth could her sister's ex want—and why wasn't he calling Jenna instead of her? "Darren? Why are you calling? Is something wrong?"

A nervous laugh. Then, "I'm sorry. I hope I'm not intruding."

What was she supposed to say? Of course he was. "Not at all."

"I wanted to give my condolences about Aunt May." Darren's words sounded stilted, rehearsed, and barely genuine.

She really should hang up. "Thank you."

"I also wanted to see how Jenna's doing. With … everything. She hasn't been back to the city, and I wanted to check in."

Ah, so there it was, his real reason for calling. Sarah resisted the urge to tell her sister's good-for-nothing ex-boyfriend that if

Jenna was interested in letting Darren know how she was doing, she'd tell him herself. Still, years of honing her diplomacy skills on the PTA board had given Sarah a better sense of propriety. "She's fine. She's renovating Aunt May's house, so keeping busy. You know how Jenna loves a project."

Like her four-year experiment with you, Sarah almost said, but didn't.

"Yes, I do. That's good to know." Darren trailed off as if lost in thought.

"Mmm." Sarah checked the clock. Three minutes had passed since she answered Darren's call. How many minutes was the proper etiquette for entertaining an awkward, unsolicited call from her sister's ex? Four? Five? She rolled her eyes. *Please not ten.*

"Wait," Darren said. "Are you talking about May's beachfront acreage? Is that the property Jenna's renovating?"

The question struck Sarah as strange, but then, Darren was strange. A little too prim, a lot too arrogant. And a realtor. Of course he'd want to talk property. "Yes. Aunt May left it to us. We're going to flip it and split the proceeds."

When he spoke again. Darren's voice had an edge of excitement. "Wow, that's a gorgeous property."

Four minutes. "Not sure what Jenna plans to do with her half, but I'm thinking about opening up a bakery with mine."

"That's a great idea. You're an amazing baker."

His words rushed out, pulling Sarah along. Sure, she'd never cared for Darren, and he'd probably tasted her confections a grand total of one time, but it was nice to be appreciated—even if it was mostly lip service. "Thank you."

Five minutes.

"The parcel," he asked. "It's gotta be, what, five acres between the ocean and the jungle. Right?"

"Something like that." She didn't actually know. Jenna would, of course, but she wasn't going to say anything which might make Darren try even harder to get in touch with her.

The line crinkled, then went clear. Darren breathed into the silence. He sounded excited. *Too* excited. "By chance, do you have anybody representing the real estate sale?"

"Not yet." Six minutes. "Darren, I'm sorry to be so abrupt, but I really—"

"I'd like to offer my services to the family. In May's honor," he added, when Sarah didn't immediately accept. "Totally commission free."

Of course he would—but why? "That's very generous, Darren. I'm not sure how Jenna would feel, but it's a very generous offer."

She could hear Darren's smile all the way from California. "You guys discuss it. I totally understand it's a family decision. But please promise me you won't sign with anybody until you hear me out."

The clock on her oven time rolled over, and Sarah felt quite confident seven minutes was more than sufficient for an unexpected phone call. Darren's offer was compelling—a commission-free sale could save them a substantial amount of money, and for all his failings as a boyfriend, Jenna had always said Darren was an excellent realtor.

"Okay, I will. Thanks for calling, Darren."

She hung up the call and looked out of the window over her kitchen sink, but if her dad was out tooling around in his workshop, Sarah didn't see him. Instead, she was wondering why Darren had seemed so interested in her aunt's property—and what an additional sum of money on the sale could do for her future bakery plans.

An offensive cracking sound followed by the noisy clatter of wood against wood ripped Jenna's attention away from the living room floorboard she was hammering into place. She managed to jerk her head up just in time to see Ben yank a second piece of crown molding off the top rim of the wall and send it clattering to the floor at his feet.

"What are you doing?" Her voice came out somewhere between surprised and impatient, but mostly exhausted. It had felt great to hold Ruby again, but between her old hammer and the sledgehammer, Jenna's arm had gotten a better workout over the past couple of weeks than it had in years. Her gaze averted from the task at hand, she misjudged her aim, sending Ruby's barrel straight down on her thumb. It smarted, and she tried to shake out the pain. "That's crown molding and it's in good condition," she said, wincing as she used her palms as levers against her knees to help her into a standing position. Another whack like that and she might lose use of the digit for a week. "We agreed we were keeping the molding."

Ben stepped down from his ladder as Jenna wiped dusty handprints on the thighs of her jeans and stretched out the kinks in her back. She'd been crawling around on the floor ever since lunch, nailing down loose floorboards and trying to keep her thoughts from wandering back to that moment on the porch a few days ago when she'd almost lost herself in Ben's eyes. Back on her feet for the first time in hours, Jenna realized how tired she felt. It was no wonder—she and Ben had been so engrossed in their work the light pouring in through the open windows had faded into the dusky tones of twilight without notice.

"And I would absolutely insist we refinish and reuse it," Ben agreed. He turned the piece of wood over in his hand, inspecting the wear and tear on the edges. "If it weren't upside down."

"Upside down?" Jenna moved closer to Ben as he turned the piece of molding he'd just ripped down and held it to the wall in the proper way.

"That's how it's supposed to sit, see?" He drew her attention to the curve of the molding and illustrated how it would fit tucked against the edge of the ceiling. "It's not supposed to be flush with the wall. It should sit on an angle—and right side up."

Seeing it for herself, Jenna realized he was right. What's more, she had no idea how she'd missed it. These were the sorts of small details an architect was supposed to know. "Right. I'm embarrassed I missed that."

Ben gave her a sympathetic look. "Happens to the best of us," he said, tossing the damaged piece of molding into the pile accumulating on the floor in the center of the room. "I have a friend who's a CEO for a huge internet shopping site. He spends a full day at the warehouse every two weeks. And he doesn't just stand around—he tapes boxes, drives the forklift, packs the truck. He feels it's necessary to see and feel his business as often as he can, and he enjoys it. He tells me all the time, if he ever found himself unemployed, he would go to the nearest warehouse and apply for a job." He leveled Jenna with a meaningful look. "He finds real satisfaction in emptying a warehouse by noon and filling it up by five."

"So, you're telling me I should moonlight as a forklift driver?"

"Hey, don't turn your nose up at forklift driving until you've tried it." Ben laughed. "You might actually like it. But no, not my point. May said you were a brilliant architect. Maybe renovating this old lady and getting your hands dirty will only make you that much better at designing new buildings."

Jenna considered his point. "One of my old professors did say the best way to learn about things was to do them."

"Absolutely. Besides, I've seen what you can do with a sledgehammer and a tin of nails. If you ever get tired of designing, reno might not make a bad second act."

Jenna made sure doubt showed on her face. "Do you believe that? I mean about your friend the warehouse CEO, not my second career in renovation."

"In a way, I live it."

"Yeah you do." Jenna smirked as she lowered back down into a squat in front of her wood pile, raised her hammer, and sent the business end of the steel-tipped object crashing down right on top of her thumb.

Hard.

Jenna screamed as pain radiated down her arm. Ruby fell to the floor, the jewel-inlaid hammer clattering at her feet and sending the small pile of nails she'd assembled scuttling in every direction.

"My thumb!" she screeched, holding her fist tightly against her chest as a hot rush of tears pushed against the backs of her eyes. She'd been daydreaming while she worked, her thoughts becoming more and more distracted as she hammered each of the nails into the wood planks. She'd nipped her thumb once or twice, but the last blow had been a full-contact *bang*. It didn't smart, it seared, and her whole body was awash with pain. "Son of a banana tree, that hurts so bad!"

"Let me see." Ben immediately stopped what he was doing and rushed over, pulling her hand into his so he could see the damage.

Somehow, Ben's touch made the pain hurt even more. "No!"

Jenna wrenched her hand back, dancing around the room in angry little hops as she tried to fan the pain out of her fingers. The tears were leaking out through her eyes now, and she clamped her eyelids shut to dam them.

Jenna felt Ben move behind her, trying to catch her like she was a butterfly evading a net. "Let me see."

"No, please leave me alone." It was hard to speak around the pain.

Growling with frustration, Ben abandoned the chase and rushed to the cooler. He plucked out the plastic baggie containing his sandwich, tossed the leftovers from his lunch out, and refilled the sack with ice cubes from the cooler. Jenna gave up on shaking the pain out of her poor finger and stuck the tip of it in her mouth, trying to suck the hurt out instead. Aunt May had taught her once how to do that with bee stings. It probably wouldn't work with hammer injuries, but she was willing to give it a try.

"Give me your hand."

She heard Ben's voice, demanding this time, somewhere behind her.

Jenna planted her feet and shook her head, still fixated on the awful sensation in her finger. The sharp sting of the pain had lessened but not diminished. It was now all the way up to her elbow. Tears had started to stream down her cheeks without her permission, and she couldn't be sure if they were from pain or embarrassment—or both. She felt Ben's hand on her shoulder and scooted away.

"No." The word came out in a whimper. She could feel her heartbeat in her thumb, and it throbbed. "It'll burn."

"Jenna." Ben sighed, his tone patient. Jenna felt the icy coolness of the plastic bag on her back as Ben planted both hands on her shoulders and spun her to face him, painfully pulsing thumb and embarrassing tears and all.

Ben seemed surprised to see the tears collected on her cheeks, but he didn't remark on them or give her one of those pandering looks men sometimes did when they saw women cry. Instead, he reached for the handkerchief in his back pocket, then shook it out and lifted it to her cheek. Very softly, he patted her tears dry. In return, Jenna allowed him to take her hand and he did, pressing the bag of ice against her thumb and inspecting her hand gingerly so as to not induce any additional discomfort.

"It doesn't look too bad. Nothing's broken, nothing's bleeding." The sharp pain in her thumb seemed to recede, leaving a powerful ache in its wake held in check by the pressure of Ben's skin against hers.

Jenna sniffed between sobs. Her eyes were still wet, but the tears had stopped. Her face flushed. "It hurts."

Ben lifted the ice bag enough to peer more closely at her injury. "The ice will prevent swelling and the cold will help the pain," he promised, looking from her thumb to her face as he spoke to make sure she was listening. His gaze caught hers and with their eyes locked, Ben leaned in and laid a chaste kiss on Jenna's thumb. The gesture felt automatic, familiar and endearing, and Jenna's breath caught in her throat.

A cool spot bloomed on her skin from where Ben's lips had touched her. From there it spread upward, chasing away the throbbing in a pleasurable flood of sensation until her heartbeat in her throat pulsed back to its rightful place in her chest. "Did you just kiss my boo-boo?"

"I suppose I did." Ben sounded surprised, and red blossomed on his cheeks.

He blinked but when his eyes reopened, his gaze was still locked on hers, and Jenna felt the same magnetic tug she had before.

The cool spot on Jenna's thumb sent shivers down her spine. "Thanks."

Still holding her hand in his, Ben drifted closer, filling the space between them. He lifted her thumb to his lips again, brushing a second soft kiss across her finger, which no longer hurt even the tiniest bit. Jenna stepped into his embrace, still gazing up into his eyes as his grip slipped from her hand and slid down her arm, landing at her elbow.

Jenna's body anchored against him, Ben's voice came out thick. "Is it feeling any better?"

Her thumb? Was it still throbbing? "I have no idea ... yes?" She cleared her throat, pulled back from the gravity of his arms. "We should get back to it."

Ben let her go, smiling. "Not with your thumb-sicle. Why don't we knock off early today? It's almost quitting time anyway." He checked his watch and ran his hand back through his hair, but looked away when she spoke. "What do you say, want to spend another meal together? I know a great place that doesn't mind the dust or sweat—or a bandaged thumb."

Was it the pain in her thumb speaking, or was he was asking her out? Either way, the offer was strangely attractive, even if it did involve going out into public looking as if she'd been rolling around in a sawmill. A matter of days ago, she'd have rather starved than eat a piece of toast with Ben Fletcher. Now, she was sad to decline the invitation. "Sarah's making dinner."

Ben waved away her apology. "Another time, maybe."

An idea sparked in Jenna's mind. "Why don't you join us?

She'd love to have you over, if you're interested."

"How do you know that?"

Jenna *wasn't* sure, but she felt confident she could bring Sarah around to the idea of feeding an extra mouth on short notice. "Because she always cooks too much food," Jenna said. "She loves to cook. She's an amazing baker, too. Besides, I'm sure she'd love to hear how the renovations are coming, and I don't think she totally trusts my opinion."

Ben hesitated, shifting nervously on his feet, but he didn't say no. "I don't want to impose on family."

"It's not an imposition. Like I said, Sarah always cooks plenty of food. But—" She gave Ben a sly smile. "My sister is less forgiving about sweat and drywall dust at the dinner table."

Ben laughed and the sound washed the look of uncertainty from his face. "Don't worry. I'll shower first."

Electricity bubbled under Jenna's skin. "So that's a yes?"

"It's a yes. I'd be happy to join your family for dinner."

The pain in Jenna's thumb was totally gone now, replaced by another sensation—excitement. "I'll call and let her know you're coming."

Chapter Eighteen

"I've had more than a few home-cooked meals in my life, but I can safely say not many were as good as this one." Ben leaned back in his chair to prove his compliment, resting both hands atop his stomach. "Everything was absolutely delicious, Sarah. Thank you for having me over."

Sarah smiled and Jenna thought it was the first genuine one she'd seen her sister give all week. Perhaps it had something to do with the fact that all the plates had been cleared and not a scrap of uneaten food remained in any of the serving dishes. The conversation around the table throughout dinner had been just as satisfying, and the array of pies Sarah had prepared for dessert made the end of the meal extra sweet.

"Thank you for joining us," Sarah said as she refilled his glass with chilled white wine. After another round of top offs, she returned the bottle to its place at the center of table. "Jenna talks about you a lot."

Ben raised an eyebrow, hiding a smile behind a sip of wine. "Oh does she?"

Jenna caught her fork before it hit the plate. "I wouldn't say a lot," she shot back. "Just whenever it's relevant—about the renovations at Aunt May's."

She glared at her sister as she sipped from her glass, hoping

Sarah could read the message written in her eyes: *shut up*.

Sarah returned a devious glance and looked as if she intended to press the matter, but Mike cleared his throat at the other end of the table and Sarah changed course. "So how's the house coming? Jenna is keeping us all in suspense with the renovations."

"It's not suspense, it's a *project*," Jenna clarified. "Sometimes there isn't much to tell—or I'm too tired to tell it, anyway. We've finished with the demolition, which was therapeutic. Who would have thought breaking down walls could feel so good? But once we got the walls down and started to open up the downstairs, everything else has been falling into place." *Sometimes literally*, she thought. She'd nearly been the victim of a collapsing chunk of sheetrock once or twice. Her thumb was still throbbing inside its mummy bandage, the temporary pain relief she'd experienced while being lost in Ben's eyes long gone.

Sarah cut at her strawberry pie, thoughtful. "I bet. The house was in pretty bad shape before Aunt May went into the home, and I know the climate hasn't done it any favors since. I can only imagine what you two must be having to do to bring it back."

Jenna shot a quick glance across the table at Ben. Oh, if she wanted, she could give Sarah a list—a long one. The truth, though, was the list was not only long, but slow. Things she'd thought would be easy fixes had a peculiar habit or becoming big chores, mostly because Ben insisted they be carried out with the utmost precision—and his idea of perfection often conflicted with hers. Then again, she wasn't exactly complaining about all the extra time they were spending together. Not yet, at least. And they were doing just fine with the budget. "Ben is a stickler on making sure everything is done just right. Maybe a little *too* much of a stickler."

"Impossible," he argued, snapping his eyes meaningfully to

her bandaged thumb. "I just have high standards."

"I can appreciate that," Mike chimed in from the head of the table. "No sense doing a job halfway."

Sarah laughed. "I don't think Jenna has ever done anything halfway in her life."

Jenna raised her glass in mock salute to her sister. *Finally.* It felt good to have Sarah back on her side, rather than harassing her about Ben.

"Oh, I believe it," Ben agreed. "She's every bit as much of a perfectionist as I am. No doubt about that." He took a bite of the pie, moaned his appreciation to Sarah as he chewed, then waved his fork between the two women. "I imagine you two were close growing up?"

Sarah and Jenna shared a look. "By some miracle, yes," Sarah confirmed.

"What do you mean?"

"I was a tomboy, always out with my dad, banging nails and finding ways to get dirty outside," Jenna explained. "Sarah was always inside baking with Mom, or gardening. We were total opposites."

"We still are," Sarah interjected. She reached across the table and gave Mike's hand a pat. "I couldn't wait to settle down and have a family of my own. Jenna wanted nothing more than to chase her dreams back to the States."

The implication in Sarah's words made Jenna bristle. It wasn't like she didn't want to settle down or have a family; both of those were definitely on her to-do list at some point. She just hadn't had the chance yet. If only Darren... *No,* she scolded herself. Breaking up with Darren Taylor had been the right decision. She had to cut her losses sometime. Still, was leaving the islands to chase her dreams really such a bad thing? Jenna didn't think so—and she was getting a little tired of asking herself the question.

"But it would have been nice if you had been in the kitchen with us more often," Sarah was saying.

Jenna blinked out of her thoughts and back to the conversation. "And it would have been nice if you had spent more time outside with me and Dad."

"I suppose." Sarah's tone had grown terse.

Jenna sensed the familiar argument looming, and directed her attention back to Ben. "Despite our *obvious* differences, my sister and I have a lot in common." Perhaps now was a good time to share the realization she'd had about why Aunt May had left her house to both sisters, and not just one. "I build and Sarah bakes, but the two things aren't really all so different. We both create beautiful things with our hands, shaping raw ingredients into something whole and complete. I think Aunt May knew that better than we did, and that's why she left her house to both of us—so we could rebuild something together. We aren't literally working on the renovation in the same way, but I'm using the skills Dad taught me, and Sarah is discovering new ways to use hers."

"May was a wise woman," agreed Ben, "maybe a little too wise, actually. She always knew how to help people see their truest selves by living every day in the spirit of Aloha. She truly was a woman of the islands. What was it she used to say—*I ka nana no a 'ike.*"

"By observing, one learns," translated Jenna. She gave her sister a wistful smile. Yep, that sounded like Aunt May.

Mike rose from his seat and began gathering dishes. "Well, in that case, I've enjoyed enough meals to have learned what comes after dessert. Who's ready for coffee?"

Ben put his napkin on the table and rubbed his palms

together. "I know I am. Here, let me give you a hand."

"Not a chance!" Sarah swatted away Ben's hand. She snatched up his plate and waved it between him and Jenna. "You two have been working hard all day, every day. Go relax out on the porch. We'll take care of this."

⁂

While Sarah and Mike tidied up the dining table, Jen and Ben retired to the back porch with their mugs. Jenna protested at first, but then Mike shooed her out of the kitchen, pushing Ben out behind her. If she didn't know better, she'd think her sister and brother-in-law were up to something.

Then again, they probably were.

Jenna sat in the two-person swing and patted the open seat, then held the bench still so it didn't rock when Ben took the space beside her. The two rocked quietly for a few moments, sipping their coffee and taking in the view as the sun set behind the Pacific. Despite growing up on the islands, Jenna had never outgrown the beauty of a Hawaiian sunset. A sky awash in brushstrokes of indigo and blue. The pointed green fingers of palms waving lazily as they painted the sky. The salty scents of ocean sprinkled on the evening breeze. Jenna let her gaze wander over the display of leafy green ferns and blooming hibiscus surrounding Sarah's back porch. She teased her sister, but Sarah truly was an incredible gardener. Just like she had their mother's aptitudes in the kitchen, Sarah had Aunt May's green thumb. Jenna's succulents were probably dead on her windowsill back in LA.

"So," Ben started after a few minutes, "how long were you and your ex together?"

"Four years." She almost asked what prompted the question, but decided against it. It didn't matter.

"That's a pretty big investment."

And you haven't even taken into account relationship equity, Jenna thought. She swallowed the grunt in her throat. "I should have known it wasn't going anywhere. I was too wrapped up in my career to see clearly, and so was he. I don't know if we fell apart or just timed out."

Ben's voice was even. "So what now?"

"Now I take it day by day. I wasn't kidding about demo day being cathartic. Honestly, I feel a little better with every wall I demolish." She meant it. Patti had once encouraged Jenna to try one of those stress programs that had you shatter dishes in a padded room. She'd thought it an utterly preposterous idea at the time, but now it didn't seem so crazy. Jenna bumped her shoulder against Ben's. Hopefully her gratitude would transfer through the touch.

He relaxed in the seat beside her. "But we're done knocking down walls," he teased, "unless you want to forego finishing the upstairs bedrooms and just sleep in the kitchen."

Jenna swallowed down a sip of coffee. "I don't plan on sleeping in the kitchen, or any other room for that matter. I'm not going to live there, remember? This is just a flip. Fix it and sell it."

Ben stiffened beside her. He cleared his throat.

"Right, I forgot. Either way, we're going to keep the rest of the walls. Please don't knock down anymore."

He leaned his head to the side so when Jenna turned to face him, she found herself staring up into his blue eyes flecked with gold. The angle was different this time, though no less arresting. Trying to ignore how handsome Ben Fletcher was, was like trying to forget the colors of a Hawaiian sunset. Impossible.

"And don't worry—" His voice had dropped to a whisper. "There will be plenty of nails to hammer in."

"Good." Sarah's head drifted closer to Ben's.

His lips were inching toward hers, so she read his next words as he said them. "Just watch your thumbs."

The sound of the backdoor opening forced them apart, pushing away from each other so quickly Ben's coffee sloshed from his mug and left a dark stain on his pant leg. Jenna felt a blush crawl up her cheeks as Sarah emerged, carrying a plate of homemade cookies.

"Who wants a snack?"

Ben's eyes bulged at the promise of something delicious. "I would love one." He reached for the plate and retrieved a cookie, then took a large bite. "That's amazing," he said, keeping his hand over his mouth so that he could talk around the confection without crumbs falling out.

"That's nothing," added Mike, stepping out behind his wife. "You should try her pineapple upside-down cake and apple cobbler."

"You should open a bakery," Ben said, helping himself to another cookie.

Sarah's face lit up. "A bakery," she echoed. "Funny you say it, because that's exactly what I intend to do."

Chapter Nineteen

"Well, what do you think?"

Sarah and Jenna were standing outside of a green and white storefront in a row of tiny shops by the beach. "Grandma's Coffee House" was stenciled on the front door, right above the *Open* sign. The wooden sign hung overhead had been freshly painted, and someone had stenciled a trellis of ivy around the doorframe, but it was clear the tiny café had seen better days. The fliers taped to the inside of the store's windows had begun to fade, and the menu still advertised holiday specials no longer in season.

"Grandma's Coffee House?" Jenna grumbled. The morning had come early—*too* early. Even the waves crashing in the distance sounded groggy. "What about it? I thought we were getting coffee?"

Exasperated, Sarah rapped her fingernail on a *For Sale* sign taped under the store's hours on the door and pushed her sunglasses up into her hairline. "We *are* getting coffee, but wake up, sis. I've been watching this place for a few years, and it just went on the market at the beginning of the year. So far, no takers, but maybe that's a sign. Maybe this could be the new home for Sarah's Bakery."

"Sarah's Bakery?" Jenna, who had forgotten her sunglasses, squinted in the early morning sun.

"Yep. I've been thinking about what we talked about, and

what I could do with my half of the sale of Aunt May's house." Sarah's grin stretched from ear to ear. "I could open my own bakery. I could actually *do* this, Jen."

Jenna took a second look at the storefront, now giving it the full weight of her attention. She could see it. Absolutely. The storefront needed a little bit of paint and polish, but it had a prime location. "It looks perfect."

Sarah beamed and swung open the front door. "Right answer. *Now* we get your coffee."

The sisters each ordered a cup of coffee and a scone at the counter, then selected a small table at the front of the bistro, near the wide picture window and the view of the beach in the distance. They discussed the café's quaint island charm while enjoying their breakfast. Even though the idea had taken her by surprise, Jenna could easily see her sister in the space—could already imagine the homey touches she'd add to the dining area, the counter spaces. New lighting would accentuate the sunshine coming in through the eastern-facing windows, maybe a new countertop—something sturdy, like granite, or quartz. Of course, Sarah would bring her green thumb to the bakery, too. The scents of her plumeria and jasmine would be enough to rival even her baked goods.

Jenna smiled. Her sister had the skills, and this little store for sale had all the curb appeal it would need to help Sarah's bakery dreams come true. "It's perfect for you, Sarah. I'm already putting in my order of blondies to go."

"You got it, Peanut," Sarah winked. "As soon as you and your handsome handyman get Aunt May's house finished, the sooner Darren can get it sold."

A bit of pastry stuck in Jenna's throat. "Wait—Darren?"

"Oh, yeah." Sarah sucked down her coffee. "He called with

his condolences about May, then offered us his real estate services to sell the house. He even offered to forgo his commission as a gift in her honor."

A thousand emotions flooded through Jenna, none of them good. Trust Darren to come sniffing around about Aunt May's property. Why hadn't Sarah told her about this before? "Sarah, tell me you didn't say yes."

Her sister winced. "Not exactly. It was more like a maybe."

A maybe? "Sarah, he's my ex!"

"I know!" Her sister put her hands up in front of her, bracing as if to ward off Jenna's ire. "And I realize it might be awkward for you, but it *was* sweet of him to offer *and* we'd save a ton in commissions with him. Doesn't that make good business sense?"

It did, but Darren always came with hidden costs, something Jenna was all too familiar with. Still, despite her personal feelings about the guy, he was an impressive realtor. Maybe she'd have a better experience being his client instead of his girlfriend.

"Yeah, I guess you're right," Jenna sighed. She just wished she could be more certain. It wasn't like Darren to offer any favors— at least not the sort that would cost him his commission. There had to be something else up his super-starched shirt sleeve, and whatever it was, Jenna wasn't sure she wanted it.

※

After breakfast, Jenna and Ben spent the better part of the morning loading up on paint supplies at the local home improvement store. Once the truck was leaden down with paint and brushes and all the other assorted items requisite to repaint an interior and exterior, they returned to tackle the house, making their way through the rooms together with the practiced movements of people who had worked together for years rather than just a few short weeks.

They finished spackling the living room before moving to the dining room, first filling cracks with the sticky white putty, and then smoothing away the excess. Ben's biceps flexed when he lugged the heavy bucket of spackle between the rooms, and Jenna spun away before he could catch her staring. She didn't let on in turn when, in the kitchen, Jenna caught Ben watching her tie her toolbelt around her waist.

In the living room, Ben held the ladder for Jenna while she used a small brush to color in the paint edges right beneath the upper crown molding—which had been reattached in the correct direction. Once the trim was done, Jenna rolled paint on one wall while Ben tackled another, the drips from their roller brushes dotting the brown paper they'd taped down to protect the new ceramic tile Ben had spent all night laying.

The names of the paint colors they'd chosen reflected the spirit of the Victorian home. It was Knight's Armor Gray for the living room, and a shade of blue called Meetinghouse for the kitchen. The travertine backsplash popped against the fresh new paint, and when Ben lifted his shirt to wipe the sweat from his brow and exposed the muscular ripples of his stomach, Jenna turned the same shade of Dusty Crimson they'd painted the dining room.

They'd squabbled over paint colors for the downstairs bath, Jenna opting for a bright jade green and Ben preferring a more romantic shade of soft, buttery yellow he insisted would make the room airier and more inviting. In the end it came down to a coin toss that Ben won, so they finished the day standing back-to-back in the small space, painting with yellow.

It's not a terrible color, Jenna considered as she rolled her brush through her last section of boring white wall. *Kind of sunny*.

Jenna turned with the roller still in her hand. Ben had also finished his section and turned at the same time, earning himself a solid line of paint across his cheek.

"Oops!" Jenna pulled her bottom lip under, biting down on it to keep from laughing. Slathering Ben in paint had been an accident, but he did look pretty dang cute with a line of yellow over his eyes and nose. Totally worth it.

Ben smeared the paint away and a coy smile crept over his lips, pressing out the dimples in his jaw. "Thanks, but it's not my shade."

Jenna laughed, then lied. "No, it's not."

"Well, you don't have to say it like that." Ben lifted his roller, his eyes widening meaningfully as he brandished the brush at her.

Instantly, Jenna knew she was in for it.

Ben lurched forward and Jenna fled from the bathroom, holding her roller in front of her as she ran through the house, avoiding Ben as he closed in behind her.

"You're right, you would look so much better in this color than I would!" he called after her as they ran in circles through the open floorplan of the house, both with paint rollers outstretched and dangerously close to smearing the wrong color paint on freshly finished walls.

"You're fired!" Jenna yelled from the dining room, watching as Ben's shadow slid into the kitchen.

"No, I'm not!" he called back, hot on her trail.

Jenna pivoted and ran for the living room. "Yes, you are!"

Ben caught up with her, cornering her between the fireplace and the ladder in the living room. She turned her head and bared her teeth playfully as he advanced on her. He'd lost his roller and, somewhere along the chase, picked up a can of leftover paint from the dining room. Dusky red paint dripped from the edges of the paintbrush bristles as he wagged the brush in a way that seemed to have a direct connection to her heartbeat, which had developed the peculiar habit of skipping a little whenever she looked at him. "Don't you dare!"

His eyebrow lifted. "Oh, I dare."

Ben was so close now she could feel the heat of his words on her skin. He lifted his brush and swiped a red mark across her cheek.

She gaped at him, and he swiped her other cheek.

"You started it, not me," he reminded her.

Jenna spied a gallon of white paint by Ben's foot and she grinned at him, evil thoughts taking over her mind. "Okay, then I'm finishing it!"

She snatched up the paint can and dumped it over Ben's head before he could stop her, then laughed until her ribs ached as Ben stood before her, dripping and sputtering.

"I can't believe you did that!" he intoned before a wily look passed over his face. He reached forward and grabbed Jenna, pulling her against him so his body pressed against hers, smothering her entire front in white.

Before she knew it, Ben's lips were on hers. Warm, soft, and slightly tacky from paint, the kiss was enough to push any concern about being covered in paint out of her mind. Paint, schmaint. Jenna put her arms around Ben's neck and kissed him back. Lifting herself onto her toes, she tightened her arms around him and kissed away all her grief over Aunt May. All her frustration over the Barrington pitch and the weeks of home renovations and manual labor she hadn't planned for. Jenna kissed Ben Fletcher until the paint on their faces began to dry and crack. Even then his palm against her face and arm wrapped around her back kept them together, as if the two of them had become a part of the house itself—as much a part of the structure as the newly installed crown molding and tile.

When they ran out of breath, Ben pulled away to gaze down at her as Jenna settled back onto her feet. Onto solid ground.

"Jenna, I—" he started.

Jenna felt his sudden departure in a gust of cool air between them, which only served to stoke the electric current racing under her skin. Her lips burned where Ben's had pressed against them, her flesh like fire where her hands still rested atop his shoulders. When was the last time she'd been kissed like that—had kissed *someone* like that?

Too long. It had been so fresh, so unexpected, Jenna needed more. She tugged on Ben's collar, drawing him back toward her.

"What?"

Unspoken words hung on Ben's lips as the sound of tires crawling up the gravel driveaway ripped their attention away from each other too soon. The pair stayed still, hoping someone had turned down the long drive by mistake and would turn around soon. Whoever it was came closer, the crunch of gravel louder with every inch forward.

What the heck? Jenna looked over Ben's shoulder at the window facing the front drive.

A shiny black airport courtesy car had just arrived in the drive. Jenna struggled to make out the driver, but then cold recognition extinguished the heat under her skin. Wearing a tropical print shirt and his face still covered in a goatee, Darren was behind the wheel.

Something thick and uncomfortable rose in her chest. What in the world was he doing here?

Chapter Twenty

Darren had just stepped one shiny black dress shoe out of his matching shiny black rental car as Jenna stormed through the front doors of the house. He looked like a tourist, dressed in slacks and a cheesy Hawaiian shirt under his suit jacket.

Scratch that. He looked like *uppity* tourist, neatly-trimmed goatee and all.

"Darren? What are you doing here?" Jenna couldn't hide the surprise in her voice—or the aggravation.

He flashed a perfect smile in her direction. "Hi, Jenna."

Jenna heard the sound of Ben's steps behind her as she withered under Darren's scrutinizing gaze. *The paint!* She held her head high and refused to feel embarrassed. Why should she? "We had an accident ... with the paint," she explained, needlessly.

A few more steps and Ben was beside her, also covered head to toe in paint. Jenna closed her eyes. Okay, even though she didn't owe her ex anything, this was still a tad awkward.

"I can see." Darren's tone was dry.

Silence.

"Darren, this is Ben Fletcher." She shot Ben a meaningful look as she nodded in the other man's direction. "Ben, this is Darren Taylor."

Understanding flashed across Ben's face. His hand lifted to his nose, wiped at the paint crusted there. "Heard a lot about you. Nice to meet you."

Ben wiped a paint-covered hand on paint-covered coveralls and stretch it toward Darren. After a few seconds hesitation, Darren emitted a choked sound and accepted the handshake. Jenna blinked to hide her eye roll. She knew exactly how Darren would feel to get his hands dirty with paint and grime. At least she wouldn't have to hear about it later.

No longer my problem, Jenna thought, and the tension in her chest loosened just a little. "Ben is renovating the house," she explained.

"With Jenna," Ben corrected. He peered at her from the corner of his eye. "We are renovating the house together."

Something about the way he said *together* made Jenna's knees weak. The feeling was short-lived, because then Darren opened his mouth.

"Oh." He gave the house's exterior a long, unimpressed review, making an effort to make sure Jenna saw his eyes settle on the scabby paint and ragged edges of several still-broken windows. The exterior would be the last aspect of the house to get its beauty makeover, a fact Darren well knew but seemed satisfied to judge their progress by now. "Well, long way to go, huh?"

Ben was stiff. His mouth tightened. "Right on schedule, actually. Another couple of days, maybe a week, and she'll be as good as new."

"I'm sure."

The two men sized each other up for a moment before Darren turned his attention to Jenna. "Jenna, could we have a minute alone please?"

She'd known it was coming, but the chance to spend any alone time with the man who'd wasted four years of her life was not at the top of Jenna's priority list. Still, she could have cut the tension between the three of them with a butter knife. Something had to give. She looked to Ben. "I'll be right back, okay?"

Ben's lips were a thin line, but he nodded. "I'll just be inside if you need me," he said.

Jenna kept her face friendly until Ben was tucked safely back inside Aunt May's. Then, she spun on her heels to glare at Darren, seething. "Now are you going to tell me why you've decided to show up at my house uninvited?"

"*Your* house?" Darren's lip twitched. "Don't tell me you're getting too comfortable out here in the tropics."

"You know what I mean." Even though she'd been counting down the days till the renovation was complete, she'd almost forgotten her ownership of the house was temporary. That was why Darren was here, after all—he hadn't come for her, but to get the house listed for a commission he was somehow willing to lose. Darren being here meant she was selling the house. It meant the renovation was done. More upsetting, it meant her time with Ben was almost over, too.

"I can see the contractors here aren't all they're cracked up to be," Darren said. He reached out and touched a spot of dried paint on Jenna's shoulder, rubbed it between his fingers like grime.

"Actually, Ben is fantastic." The words were poison on Jenna's lips. "The spilled paint was on me."

Darren's lip twitched again. "Got it," he said. "Anyway, Sarah told you about our call, right? About me helping to sell the property?"

"Yes, and it's very generous." Jenna bit the words off. "But the house isn't ready yet, and we could have done this over the phone,

Darren."

Over the phone. They could have done it by mail.

"That's true, but I can't deny actually wanting to see you again. To present my proposal in person."

Proposal? Darren's choice of vocabulary sent sparks through Jenna's limbs.

Darren took a step forward. Jenna took a step back. "It's a little late for proposals."

He stopped moving. "I deserve that, and you were right about a lot of what you said when we broke up. But I think I found a way to fix everything."

Fix everything? How did showing up unannounced with an offer fix *anything?* She rolled her eyes. "You're just here to sell the house."

Darren had the grace to look sheepish. "Selling the house was the first plan, but then I had another idea that's even bigger—and one that might even help put me back in your good graces, too."

"What do you mean?"

"Paradise," Darren said, brandishing his trademark realtor smile. "Paradise for three dozen families."

A beat passed as Jenna stared at Darren. The words she understood, but they didn't make sense. What paradise?

Darren put his arm around Jenna's shoulders and turned their bodies so they faced the wide green expanse of May's property. Green, wild, trimmed by jungle and ocean. "Think about it. These five acres of prime oceanfront are worth a fortune—way more here than even in LA. They could be the condo project we never got to build. And I've talked Orville Barrington into backing us. He's in love with the idea—even with a higher price tag."

"What do you mean backing *us?*"

"You and me," Darren clarified. "We build it together. You design, I sell. We do our own version of Terrace Pines right here."

Jenna considered the landscape adjustments she'd already made to her model, the sustainability plans, the green living. Most of it checked out but— "There are no pine trees in Hawaii."

"Okay, so Terrace Pineapple or Mango Terrace, or whatever you want to call it. The point is, your whole family can benefit from May's inheritance in more ways than you imagined. Instead of flipping this house, it becomes an investment. A big one. Sarah gets her bakery—"

"How do you know about that?" Jenna cut in.

Darren laughed. "I know your family, Jenna. I was part of your life for four years."

The use of past tense stung, even though it shouldn't. Maybe it was because he was twisting timelines, mixing past with future when she wasn't even totally sure of the present. She twisted out of Darren's grasp and stepped away, out of his reach. Darren's idea, although compelling, was impossible. Did he truly expect her to turn her aunt's home into a condominium complex? After all the blood, sweat, and actual bruises she'd put into the renovations so far?

Then again, if she'd been fine with fixing the house up to sell Aunt May's legacy, wouldn't it be better to put her stamp on it, too?

"Take the number you have in your head from the sale and multiply it by a hundred. Your dad could do a world tour of all the best surfing spots, and Emma could get a real start in life and not have to go through years of trying to figure things out like you did," Darren added, helpfully.

"True," Jenna admitted, "but strangely unnerving coming

from you."

Darren spread his hands out in front of him. "Think about the opportunity. You get to design a destination community *exactly* the way you would love to. Everything you saw for Terrace Pines and more. All here."

Jenna shook her head, trying to break loose the dozens of thoughts all vying for her attention. The vision Darren had painted before her was almost too good to be true. Sure, he was a little overzealous and there was no denying his selfish motives, but he also wasn't wrong. Aunt May's beachfront property was valuable—very valuable—and nothing she could do to renovate the home would ever bring the sale value to anything close to what the land itself was worth. If she accepted Darren's offer, not only would she be able to finally pursue her dreams and prove she had what it took to be the architect she always wanted to be, but her family would all reap the benefits. Sarah would get her bakery, the kids a start in life, and her dad could take Betty Lou on the road—all due to a little bit of real estate savvy and Aunt May's gift.

Aunt May. She had entrusted her last worldly possessions to Jenna, but was this what she would have wanted? How much of her will was about the house, and how much was about helping her family see their true potential—to follow their dreams?

"It's not about what I get," Jenna decided finally. "It's about my family, and Aunt May."

The left corner of Darren's lip pulled. "You mean her legacy, right?"

Legacy. Jenna looked over her shoulder at the house. She could see Ben's outline as he worked, coating the last unfinished wall in a layer of fresh paint.

"Well, it's pretty hard to imagine Aunt May not wanting the

best for all of you," Darren said. "Don't you think your family never having to worry about money again is a legacy she'd be proud of?"

"I never thought of this property as condos before, but you're right. It would be a game-changer for my family. It's still Aunt May's property, and with a structure like that so many people could love the land as much as she did." Jenna let the thought settle. Something was out of place, and it wasn't what to do with the structure on her aunt's land. "And you? What do you get out of it?"

The obvious answer flared in her thoughts. Money, of course. And a lot of it. "I thought you were offering to forego your commission?"

Darren had the decency to look embarrassed. "On the sale of the house, yes, but Jenna … this is a whole different deal. It's not about commission, it's about *potential.*"

Jenna took a step backward, but Darren reached out and took her hand. "I won't deny it. We spent four years trying to build a nest egg together, and an opportunity like this would be a financial game-changer for me, too. For both of us."

Jenna scoffed. Right. Relationship equity. She'd nearly forgotten. "You've always been about the deal."

Her words were cold, but Darren was quick to warm them up. "Not since you left. I've been trying to see things the way you do."

"What—*sunny?*"

Darren flinched. Recovered. "That was a stupid thing to say. I'm really sorry about that."

It was the sincerest apology Jenna thought she'd ever heard Darren give. It didn't change anything, but at least it made her feel a tiny bit better. "I have to get back … but I'll think about it, okay?"

"Absolutely," Darren promised. His face lit up again with his trademark smile and he adjusted his suit jacket over his Hawaiian shirt. "I'll be on the island a few more days. I have the paperwork drawn up if you want to move forward. This could all happen fast. You could start revising your Terrace Pines blueprint, and Barrington has his private jet on standby the moment you say yes."

Before Jenna could say anything, Darren leaned it and laid a quick kiss on her cheek. It itched like mango sap and she lifted her hand to scratch at the spot as she watched Darren wave goodbye, slip back behind the wheel of his rental car, and drive away.

Chapter Twenty-One

Jenna's head was still spinning minutes later when she made her way back into the house.

"Everything okay?" Ben asked.

Yes? No? Maybe? Jenna wasn't sure. "Can we call it a day?"

"Not like you to shut down early." His eyebrows scrunched together and he pointedly didn't look to see if Darren's car was still in the drive. "Schedule and all."

A sudden urge to spill the beans about Darren's offer filled Jenna's mouth. She swallowed it. "I know, I just ... I need to talk with Sarah and my dad."

"What did he say?"

He. Darren.

Apparently Ben knew how to read between the lines and not just paint within them. "Darren has an investment group that wants the whole property for a condo development," she said, deciding to skim on details and just stick with the facts. "Actually, it's *my* development. A big pitch in LA I lost. The investor has ... reconsidered."

"What about finishing the house?"

Jenna winced. "There would be no need. If we go with the condo plan, we'll have to just demo it to the ground."

"And you'd be okay with that? After all the work we've done?"

The note of incredulity in his voice sharpened Ben's words.

"Financially, it would mean a whole new life for my family—the whole family. Me too. My feelings don't really matter. I have to think about everyone else."

"And what about May?" he countered. "What about what she hoped for with this renovation?"

"Ben, Aunt May left it up to me to figure out what to do with the property. And that's exactly what I'm trying to do. I was always going to sell it."

"Let's keep working."

Jenna took a look around the rooms before her. They'd long since finished the demo process and begun the actual renovation, and, though the house was gutted and still unfinished, the potential was obvious. The house was going to be beautiful when they were done—and it wouldn't take long to get her there now. She peered at Ben, not sure how to respond.

The crunch of another set of tires on gravel saved her from telling him what was on her mind—that it would all be for nothing if she decided to tear it all down.

Ben's voice was hard. Distant. "The floors are here."

Outside, a large trailer truck stood with its rear doors open as two men unloaded several boxes of long wooden planks and set them on the soft green grass. By the time Jenna and Ben made it out the front door and down the steps, several boxes were waiting, and one of the men was busy organizing delivery paperwork on his clipboard.

Ben nodded at the driver and reached for the paperwork while Jenna squatted to inspect the wood. "Is this laminate?"

"This is the real deal," Ben said. "This is genuine oak hardwood. Taken care of, it will last forever."

Numbers tallied up in Jenna's head as she did the math on the cost of hardwood versus laminate. It wasn't pretty. Regardless of what she decided to do about Darren's offer, unexpected expenses would topple her budget if she didn't keep them in check. Aunt May had left enough funds to cover the renovation, but not to rebuild the whole home from scratch—and the more the put into a renovation, the more they stood to lose in a demolish. "I said I wanted laminate. It's half the price."

Ben shot her one of those crooked looks that only looked cute when she wasn't frustrated with him making decisions that were contrary to what she'd asked for. "We said we'd table it for later. Laminate won't match the wood that's already down," he explained. "If you want to do laminate, you'd have to replace the whole floor, which would eat into the savings you're worried about. Either way, we come up pretty even."

"Nobody will know the difference!" Jenna exclaimed. Of course Ben had circumvented her wishes with his almighty commitment to thoroughness. It wasn't as if this was his bank account.

"We will."

Jenna's irritation morphed into anger. "It's not *your* house. You're the contractor. You work for me, remember?" A sour taste welled on Jenna's tongue. Now she was quibbling over five percent instead of ten in *her* budget. She swallowed down the taste of irony.

Ben's posture went rigid, his pen frozen on the signature line. His voice had gone from edgy to sharp to razor fine. "I see. I'm sorry, Jenna. I thought you would be happy."

"Send it back."

A second truck pulled into the drive and Jenna moved away without bothering to wait for Ben's response. Her dad cut the engine and climbed out of his truck, noticing the wood. He gave Jenna a one-armed hug and spoke over her shoulder. "That's nice wood flooring."

Jenna sighed. The last thing she needed right now was to find herself outnumbered about flooring. "We're pretty busy, Dad."

Jim's gaze shifted from the wood to Ben, who was still holding the clipboard with a look of fierce determination on his face. Jenna shot him one back.

"I brought us some lemonade," her dad said, nudging her back toward the house—toward a neutral zone. "Come on."

Instead of going in through the front doors and trampling over their construction mess, Jenna led her dad around the large property and into the backyard. The buzzing sound of Ben's power tools was barely audible somewhere in the distance, and Jenna sincerely hoped he'd sent the hardwood back and hadn't hurried up and started installing it while she was distracted.

"What's on your mind, Peanut?" Jim asked, settling at the small sitting table Aunt May had kept in the now-overgrown garden. He pulled out the thermos of lemonade he'd brought with him, then unscrewed the cap and pulled out the collapsible cups to pour a glass for him and Jenna.

Jenna accepted her cup and took a sip. "How do you know something's on my mind?"

"Thirty years of being your father," he quipped. "Not to mention the look on your face. You're rattled, and I think it's over more than those floors, which I also know you're not happy about."

Jenna leaned back in her chair with a sigh. The truth was, the floors themselves were the least of her worries right now. Honestly, she was more agitated with Ben disregarding her request than the hardwood itself. It wasn't as if they'd made a firm decision not to use it, and hardwood *would* look better, even if it was more expensive. Even if they tore the whole place down. The other things that had gone wrong in Jenna's life, though, weren't so easily fixed—there were no line items for broken promises and failed dreams, not even if Darren was dangling a very attractive carrot in front of her with the Terrace Pines deal.

"What's not on my mind?" Jenna said, when she realized she'd gotten caught up in her thoughts and forgotten to answer the question. "I thought I would be married by now, with a couple of kids and a successful career. Not single and rebuilding"—she motioned toward the house and all it represented—"my childhood one brick at a time."

Her dad harrumphed beside her. "A house on a lake, a condo on the beach. Maybe a helicopter to shoot you back and forth," he teased, filling in Jenna's perfectly work-life-balanced daydream.

"Exactly."

Jim chuckled and Jenna couldn't help but laugh with him. Put that way, it was a pretty funny juxtaposition—especially when she was currently covered in spackle and paint and sipping lemonade with her dad in the suburbs.

"Seriously, though," Jenna went on, "my condo is small, my career is full of disappointments, and instead of planning my wedding, I was just dumped by the guy I've been with for four years. Things aren't exactly going according to plan. Not even a little. And don't even get me started on *this*." She waved her hands about to include the house, Ben. All of it.

"Maybe someone's trying to tell you something." Jim drained his cup and set the empty container on the table. He levelled a meaningful look at his daughter. "Are you listening?"

Jenna felt her lips pull back in a grimace. "The message I'm getting is 'life is all about making the choices that have the least amount of destructive side effects.'"

Her dad sighed and looked back toward the house. "Nothing is perfect, Jenna. Not even love. But when you find the right person, it's pretty darn close. It's all about figuring out what you want as opposed to what you think you want."

"You're not nearly as subtle as you think you are, you know."

Jim laughed and the sunlight reflected in his eyes. "Not trying to be."

"What do you want, Dad?"

He put his finger to his lips, turning his gaze away from the house and up to the sky as he considered his response. Jenna waited a beat, finding herself enjoying the quiet hum of power tools and the aftertaste of the lemonade. She had to admit that her current predicament wasn't where she'd expected to find herself—not even close—but it had its charms, too.

After a few long seconds of deep thought, Jim poured them both a second glass of lemonade. Raising his cup in a toast to hers, he said, "I want to finish my darn table."

Chapter Twenty-Two

"It's kind of amazing," Sarah said as she refilled her teacup for the third time then took another bite out the half-eaten, orange-glazed scone set on the plate before her. "Grandma's Coffee House, here I come."

Jenna leaned back in her chair and sighed, her own cup of tea untouched. The tray of treats on the table before her looked appetizing as always, but the thought of sugar made her stomach turn. She did a quick survey around the kitchen table, glancing from her sister's look of unbridled enthusiasm, to her niece's expression of shock, and her brother-in-law's blank stare. Aside from the obvious visions of sugarplums and small business ownership dancing through her sister's head, everyone else at the table seemed stunned into silence. Her father hadn't said a word. Ethan had been too preoccupied with video games to join the family meeting.

Daddy hasn't even blinked, Jenna considered. He hadn't, had he? The whole time she had presented the details of the offer Darren had emailed over, Jenna had watched her father over the top of her papers. He hadn't taken tea or pastry. He hadn't fidgeted or moved in his seat, hadn't provided any glimpse into what he might be feeling on his otherwise usually expressive face.

She could relate. When she'd first read the offer Darren had sent from Barrington's client, Jenna had been just as surprised as everyone else. Luckily she'd had the benefit of delivering the deal to insulate her from getting too wrapped up in the implications of what accepting Barrington's offer would mean. Nothing muffled feelings like paperwork; it was hard to get too tangled in the weeds of emotions when you were busy fixating on making sure you didn't miss any of the important details. Now that she was through hiding behind paperwork, though, the magnitude of the decision beared down on her full force again.

Was tearing down the house she'd nearly brought back to life really what she wanted?

The truth was, every time Jenna thought she had absorbed the brunt of this turn of events—had really taken everything in, gathered her thoughts, and made her way to a comfortable place—she blinked and the world was upside down again. Inheriting Aunt May's house had been one thing. Renovating it, another. But demolishing it, even if it was to build her dream project and give her family a better financial future than they could have dreamed of, was something else entirely—even if the price tag on the deal had more zeros than Jenna had ever seen in one string of numbers.

Emma was the first to break the silence. "So, if I pick up my grades the last two years of high school and wanted to go to the mainland to the private college of my choice, this means I could?"

Jenna didn't meet her father's gaze. "You could."

"And after that, I could get an apartment in New York and date a struggling artist with dreams of becoming the next Andy Warhol?" Emma's voice had risen an octave, the threat of a giggle crescendo hanging in the balance between her words.

"One fantasy at a time, young lady." Sarah cut in. "Let's focus on getting you through high school first."

Emma snatched up another scone, bit off one corner. "Okay, Mom."

Jenna exchanged a smile with her sister across the table. *It's hard to be so conflicted when everyone else is so excited*, she thought. Everyone, of course, except her dad. "So, I guess it's settled, then?" she started, then paused and sucked in a deep breath. "Dad, you've been kind of quiet. Penny for your thoughts?"

Jim Burke exhaled at the end of the table. He shook his head slowly, opened and closed his mouth. Finally, he cleared his throat. His voice came out thick. "May left the house to you girls. This has to be your decision." He swallowed and cleared his throat again. "See you guys later. I'm going to get back to work."

Without another word, he pushed himself to the table and headed for the back door. He pulled it open and slipped through into the dusky twilight.

"Well, that was a little odd, right?" Sarah asked. "Even for Dad?"

Jenna put her papers down on the table and crossed her hands on top of them. "I knew he'd be hesitant about this. I mean," she added, ruefully, "I'd be lying if I said I wasn't a little blown away myself. But we'd always knew we'd sell Aunt May's house once the renovation was complete. This way we're losing the house, but giving May's property a new way to live on—right?"

She sighed. Who was she asking, her sister or herself?

"I'll go talk to him," Mike volunteered. "Maybe it's a man-to-man type of thing."

All three women at the table shot him the same look. *Yeah right.*

"I'll go," said Jenna. "It's our house, but Darren and the Barrington deal are because of me, good or not. I should be the one to talk to Dad."

She pushed back from the table, stuffed a scone in her mouth, and headed outside. When Jenna arrived in her father's workspace, he was busy putting the finishing touches on the last of the kou coffee table legs, his back to her. Two had already been attached, and the remaining pair waited, freshly stained and sanded. Jim picked up one of the legs and turned it over in his hands, studying it carefully.

"Dad?"

He didn't answer.

Jenna felt her pulse in her throat. "Dad, I need you to talk to me."

Her father continued to examine the table leg in his hands, enrapt. He sniffed but kept quiet.

"I miss her too, Dad."

After another long stretch of silence, Jim sat the table leg on his workbench and turned to face her. His eyes were glassy, and there was a softness to him Jenna had never noticed before—the kind that didn't come with age. Grief clung to his skin. It pulled down his features, heavied his movements until they looked slow, strenuous.

"This table was meant to go in May's room at the retirement home," he said. "Bring a piece of her house—of the island—to her there. I started working on it a few years ago. Then other projects got in the way. Took priority. By putting it off, I was never able to give it to her before she died."

Jenna understood. Time had a way of sneaking up on you, running out before you even realized the clock was ticking. This was a lesson she'd learned all too well over the past few weeks that she'd been home. "Dad, it's not your fault. That stuff happens.

May would have understood."

"She would have," Jim agreed. He ran a large hand across the smooth surface of the coffee table. "But I'm going to finish it anyway. We need something to remember that old house by. To remember her."

"Yeah, we do." Jenna's thoughts flashed to the kou tree she'd added to her Terrace Pines models on the day of the Barrington pitch—a moment which seemed so long ago now. Had it been Aunt May in that moment, giving her one last nudge in the right direction?

Jim used his shirt to wipe away dampness at the rims of his eyes. "Just so you know, I don't need the world surfing tour. I got everything I could ever want right here." The left corner of his mouth curved into a small smile. "You and your sister are my *aloha*. Always will be."

Something tightened in Jenna's chest. "I hope the condo project is the right choice." She didn't say the rest—that accepting Barrington's lucrative offer wasn't half as attractive as painting walls and grouting tile with Ben Fletcher.

"You have your Aunt May with you always. And your mom, too. Both of them were smarter than I ever will be, and so are you."

Her father's vote of confidence warmed her heart.

"*A'a i ka hula, waiho i ka maka'u i ka hale,*" she said. May's wise words. Dare to dance and leave the shame at home.

"I couldn't agree more, Peanut," Jim said as he wrapped his arms around Jenna's shoulders and pulled her into the tightest hug he'd given her in years.

Chapter Twenty-Three

With her laptop still on the fritz, Jenna had texted Ben to let him know the family would be accepting Barrington's offer. That had been two days ago. He still hadn't texted back, and Jenna hadn't been out to the house to see if he was still hanging around working on the last few renovations. She'd wanted to— she'd even started to drive out to Aunt May's a handful of times. But every time she'd turned around. She'd told Ben to pack his tools and go home. What would she do if she found him there? More to the point, how would she feel if she didn't?

Jenna smoothed down her skirt and stepped back to examine herself in the mirror. For the past several weeks, she had traded in her usual wardrobe of business chic pantsuits and high heels for dingy overalls and paint-spackled tank tops. She'd gone so long with messy ponytails and dirty fingernails she almost didn't recognize her reflection—the girl staring back at her in the mirror wearing a floral blue and pink sundress. But there Jenna stood, looking perfectly refreshed in a tropical print dress, her hair soft around her shoulders. She swabbed a sheen of light pink gloss across her lips and draped a simple white orchid lei over her shoulders. Today was a day for celebration, and such important occasions required special accessories. The lei had been May's.

It's like I never left the islands, she thought. Jenna's heart fluttered. Her mirror reflection certainly looked the part on the outside, but her insides hadn't quite caught up. Today was the day she'd been anticipating for months; the day she finally got her name on the dotted line of an architectural project bearing her design. But it was also the day she signed away Aunt May's property, and the moment was bittersweet.

A knock on the bedroom door. Jenna brushed her skirt down again and smoothed her hair, put on her best smile. "Come in."

Emma flounced into the room, wearing short-cropped denim shorts and a breezy linen top. She plopped onto the guest bedroom, settling Jenna's laptop on the bed beside her. She flipped open the cover and booted the machine up.

"The spinning pinwheel of death means you need to clean out your laptop more than once every decade," Emma teased. "Your hard drive was full of digital garbage and it was slowing everything down. It's the reason your email program was being finicky. You're lucky the whole thing didn't crash—or catch on fire."

Sweet relief. Keeping up with emails on her phone was inconvenient at best, impossible at worst—especially when the island Wi-Fi got glitchy. Half the time she couldn't even open them, and she could forget actually accessing any attachments. "So it's fixed?" Relief swept through Jenna.

Emma beamed. "It's fixed." She pulled her cellphone out of her back pocket, did a double take at the time, and scurried off the bed. "You better hurry up and get ready. We don't want to be late."

Jenna watched the bedroom door swing shut behind her niece. Emma looked so much like Sarah when she'd been that age, but between her knack for punctuality and her big dreams of pursuing her fantasies off the island, the girl sure had a lot of her Aunt Jenna running through her veins.

Her laptop sat open before her, waiting. Jenna sucked in a deep breath. A mailbox full of work emails she could handle, but one name had been haunting her thoughts from the top of the inbox. Jenna launched her email program and scrolled down the feed until she saw Aunt May's name. She clicked the video attachment, waited for the media to load, and then put her hand over her mouth to keep her heart from spilling out when her aunt appeared on screen.

Aunt May sat on the porch of her retirement home, wearing the same clothes she'd been wearing on her last video call with Jenna.

"Jenna, there was something I wanted to say earlier, but I held back because I don't ever want you to think I'm interfering with your life," the old woman said on video. "But after we finished, I kicked myself. Of course I want to interfere; you're my little peanut."

Heaviness pushed inside Jenna's eyes and she sucked her lips under, biting down hard with her teeth. She felt her jaw tremble and she sniffed, keeping her gaze locked on the screen.

"So here goes," Aunt May continued. "When it comes to love, don't ever settle for less than what you deserve. True love is more than a practical choice, Jenna. Don't worry about being pragmatic, on schedule, and under budget. Worry about making your heart *dance*, my girl. I pray God brings you a man who will love and cherish you—not for what you can give him, but for who *you* are. I know I'm biased, but you are a very special young lady who is going to change the world with your gifts. You deserve someone who sees that in you, just like I do."

She paused to check her watch, then clicked her tongue. "Oh no, I'm late to meet your daddy for lunch. I gotta go. Goodbye for now." May looked at the screen and blew Jenna a virtual kiss. "I love you, Peanut."

The old woman leaned forward, fumbled with the camera, and the feed went dead.

It took Jenna several minutes to realize she was sobbing. These were her aunt's final words to her—words of wisdom, and hope, and love. How she wished May had shared this message on their video call! But, Jenna considered, would she have heard it so clearly then? Would it have meant as much in the moment as it did now?

No, Jenna decided as she pulled a pillow from the bed to blot her tears. *No, May's timing was perfect.* This was exactly what she needed to hear, and exactly when she needed to hear it.

⁂

When Mike pulled the car into the gravel drive of Aunt May's estate, Darren's rental was already parked outside. Jenna noticed Orville Barrington had arrived, punctual as ever. He and Darren stood side by side, in matching blazers and matching goatees, admiring the view of the ocean.

Jenna rolled her eyes. *Curb appeal.*

Jim Burke pulled up in his pickup and brought the rusty old heap to a squealing halt beside Mike's car. As Jenna, Sarah, Mike, Emma, and Ethan poured out of the Maxwell family vehicle, he cinched down a tarp covering the cargo bed.

Jenna was just about to ask what he had in the back of his truck when Sarah grabbed her elbow, pulling her toward the house. Her voice was breathy with excitement.

"I thought you said you stopped working on the house?"

"We did," Jenna responded. Then she looked at the house and the ground nearly fell out from beneath her.

Aunt May's house stood before them in all her full glory, as beautiful as Jenna had ever seen it. The cracked and broken windows were repaired, and the sagging front steps reset. The house had been painted a soft shade of pale yellow the same hue as the setting sun, offset by shutters stained the deep navy of the sky over the ocean at night. Delicate gingerbread trim in eggshell white furled along the eaves and raced up and down every angle of the home's peaks and borders. Even the front landscaping had been pruned and brought back to life. Bright red hibiscus and heliconia bloomed between long, leafy fingers of fern and palm. The gravel leading up to the house's front porch was new, too—all white shell and sand. Even the bright midday sun shining over the house's roof seemed to cast a spotlight on May's beautifully restored Victorian.

"I don't think Aunt May got the memo," Sarah breathed.

It took Jenna a few tries to find her voice. "Neither did Ben."

"Wow." Mike pointed toward the side of the house, where Ben was loading his tools into the back of his construction truck. Evidence of this morning's exterior work lay scattered about on the ground beside him—leftover pieces of trim, a half-emptied bag of potting soil, an assortment of leftover tools.

By the looks of it, Jenna and her family—as well as Darren and Barrington—had arrived just in time for the grand reveal. "I don't understand why he finished the interior," Jenna mumbled under her breath.

Her breath caught in her throat when Ben's gaze caught hers, but whatever he was thinking, his poker face revealed nothing. She tried to communicate with him with just her eyes. What was going on? Why had he finished the house?

Jenna was so busy trying to telepathically interrogate Ben, she didn't hear the crunch of polished dress shoes behind her.

"Hello, family!" Darren's voice was loud—booming—and far too cheerful for Jenna's taste.

She turned her attention to the men behind her, then stifled a scoff. Both Darren and Orville Barrington looked so out of place amongst the laid-back tropical landscape it was almost comical. Their crisp Hawaiian print shirts were too starched, their blazers too warm for the summer weather. Even their matching goatees looked too precise to be anything other than markers of city slickers desperately trying to blend in with the rest of the tourists.

Of course, Jenna reminded herself, *this is business, not vacation.*

Barrington kept his arms crossed while Darren brandished his trademark smile. He stuffed a file folder full of paperwork under his arm, then offered his hand first to Sarah, then Mike, and, finally, to Jim.

"Mr. Burke," Darren exclaimed. "Wonderful to see you again."

Jim was gruff. "Darren."

Darren extended a handshake, and Jenna watched as her father's oversized paw enveloped Darren's smaller hand. She saw Darren's realtor smile tense, then strain, as her father's grip tightened. She smiled. *Good.*

When Jim finally released Darren from the handshake, the younger man had to shake out his hand a few times. Jenna's smile widened.

Never one for pleasantries, Barrington turned his attention to Jenna. She corralled her grin into something more professional, and straightened her posture. "Mr. Barrington," she started, "this is my dad, Jim Burke, my sister Sarah, and her husband Mike and their children, Emma and Ethan."

Barrington nodded politely at each of the names in turn, but the motion was all business. When the introductions were finished, Barrington swept his hand around the property. He gestured to the beach, the jungle wrapping around the edges of May's land—everything, Jenna noticed, *except* the house.

"This is one of the most beautiful properties I could ever hope to develop," Barrington said. "I'm glad to see there are no hard feelings between us about Terrace Pines."

Just a sunny five percent, Jenna thought. She pulled her shoulders back and blinked the memory away. "No, sir."

"Jenna would never burn bridges in a business relationship," Darren contributed helpfully.

Barrington's lip twitched and Jenna wondered if he was thinking the same thing she was—*shut it, Darren.*

"Glad to hear it," he said.

The not-so-subtle note of sarcasm in his voice seemed to confirm Jenna's theory. Tension in her shoulders relaxed, but something else stirred in her belly—something warm and decidedly unfriendly. How could these two men truly not see the beauty of the home? Were they both really so obsessed with the commercial value of something that they didn't see the inherent beauty of it? A magnificently restored home stood before them—a home loved by so many—and there was no doubt in Jenna's mind the only things running through Darren Taylor and Orville Barrington's heads were dollar signs, and all the money this deal would make when they turned May's gardens into condos.

What was worse—only a mere few weeks ago, Jenna might have been thinking the same things herself.

Her stomach twisted, turned sour. How could she have been so blind, so dismissive?

Darren leaned in close to Jenna, pointing a suspicious finger to Ben's work truck. "I thought your contractor had already wrapped up his work?"

The way he said *contractor* sounded an awful lot like *boyfriend*. Jenna neither liked the implication, nor the fact that she and Ben were not currently on speaking terms. The sour feeling in her stomach crawled up into her chest. "I did, too."

Barrington cleared his throat. He motioned toward the file of paperwork in Darren's hand. "Well, shall we all do this?"

Darren shot Barrington a confirming glance and shifted away from Jenna, deftly opening his file and spreading out a thick stack of paperwork on the hood of the Maxwell's car. Everyone gathered around—everyone except Jim and Jenna. Jenna glanced at her father, but he didn't make eye contact. Were his feet suddenly as heavy as hers were?

"Mr. Barrington and I have already signed where we need to," Darren said as he pulled a ballpoint pen from his pocket and clicked it open. "So we'll just need Sarah and Jenna to sign."

He turned to Sarah. Brandished another showstopping smile. "Sarah, how about you first?"

Sarah looked for Jenna at her side, then turned an impatient glance over her shoulder where Jenna stood behind her. She mouthed a silent squeal, and then accepted then pen from Darren's proffered fingers and quickly signed her name as Darren guided her through the pages. Jenna counted the signatures, the sourness in her chest moving further up her throat with each pen stroke.

"Here." Sarah signed. One inch.

"Here." Sarah signed. Two inches.

"And here." Sarah signed. The taste was in Jenna's mouth now.

Then her sister turned and smiled back at the house. "Aunt

May would have loved this house," she said.

The taste coated Jenna's tongue as emotion threatened to rush through her lips. She nodded at her sister and turned back to the house. Her eyes swept to Ben's truck, but he was no longer there.

Finished signing, Sarah prepared to hand the pen to Jenna, but Darren intercepted.

"I brought Jenna her own special pen to sign with." He pulled a pen case from his pocket and handed it to Jenna with a flourish.

A special pen? There was something in Darren's smile that Jenna didn't recognize. No, she did recognize it, she just hadn't seen it in a very long time. How long had it been since Darren looked at her like that—like she was special, like he only had eyes for her?

She accepted the pen case and flipped it open. Inside was a thin gold fountain pen. Atop the pen, on the cushion of black velvet, was a perfect princess-cut engagement ring—a large round diamond, set on a delicate band the same shade of gold as the pen. Somehow, Jenna was able to push past the terrible taste in her mouth to speak.

"Darren … what is this?"

"My amends to you." He dropped to one knee in front of her, reaching out for her hand. "I didn't want to ruin the surprise."

Jenna clicked the box shut. She took a step back, away from Darren. He could *not* be serious. "You are unbelievable."

Before she could elaborate on what a shady, weaseling, opportunistic jerk he was, Barrington cut in. "What is happening here?"

The sarcasm in his voice had been replaced by something between bewilderment and irritation, with a healthy dose of impatience. Jenna could relate.

Darren rebounded up to his feet in a blink. Clearly, this was not going as he'd expected. "Mr. Barrington, please indulge me—"

Unfortunately, he was barking up the wrong tree. Barrington's eyes narrowed. He put a heavy hand down on top of the unfinished pile of paperwork on top of the car, as if to say, "we're in the middle of business." The unsaid words were loud enough to cause all four Maxwells to take a step backward. Ethan even looked up from his game.

"You're proposing to the sunny girl?" Barrington's voice was incredulous, unapproving. "During a deal?"

Sunny. "What did you call me?" The words rushed out of Jenna's mouth before she could stop them, and now her voice was just as hard and aggravated as Barrington's. Her left foot stepped forward, bringing her one step closer to the imposing man—and one step farther from Darren.

Darren, quick to de-escalate, pivoted, but the look on his face was anything other than confident. He spread his hands between his client and his would-be bride and blinked too fast, obviously trying to figure out the right thing to say to keep both his commission and his proposal from falling off the proverbial table.

"Uh, Jenna, sweetheart, I thought this would be a romantic way to start our new partnership," he said, lamely. "And *restart* the rest of our life together."

"We don't have a relationship anymore," Jenna snapped back. She was still angry, but the bile in her throat was receding, being washed away by a strange new sense of calm. Darren's posturing had taken him out of her line of sight and given her a much better view: Aunt May's house. *Her* house. She let the image sink in, let herself truly see the house as a home and not just a project for the first time. Thinking back through the past several weeks, she thought about every nail, every piece of tile and strip of grout she'd lovingly poured into May's home. Every new cabinet, every new swatch of paint. She'd spent so long chasing the dream of designing new, sustainable homes, that never had she considered how much joy was to be found in restoring them. Giving things a second chance was more sustainable than all the solar panels and aesthetic "green" touches she could dream up—it made them evergreen.

This is it, she realized. *This is home. My second act.*

She caught her father's eyes, and he gave her the only approval she needed—a shaka sign, a wink, and a nod.

Darren was less supportive. "But we could," he wheeled, trying to redirect her attention back to the closed pen case in her hand. He leaned in closer to whisper suggestively in her ear. "We could be partners in every way."

Jenna was firm. "No, we can't, Darren."

"Why not?"

"Because I didn't realize until just now, but I already have a partner."

Darren looked shellshocked as she handed him back the case and turned to Barrington. "Mr. Barrington, my apologies for Darren bringing you all the way out to Hawaii for nothing." She bit her lip and dared a glance at her sister. "Sarah, I will find some other way to help you get your dream. I promise." She looked to Emma. "You too, Emma."

Sarah steeled her back and gave a nod. Emma took her mother's hand and nodded too. Jenna would have laughed if she wasn't busy mustering up all of her courage for what she had to say next. She lifted her chin, channeled her best Patti Murray—hoped her faraway mentor didn't disown her for this—and delivered her final decision.

"The deal is off," she told Barrington. "I am not selling this property."

Chapter Twenty-Four

"Jenna, please." The panic was evident in Darren's voice. This was *so* not going to plan.

Barrington's voice deepened into thunder. "I could so sue you for this," he threatened.

Jenna sucked in a deep breath, held it, thought about Aunt May, and let the air in her mouth loose. She inhaled the scent of saltwater, filled her lungs with sunshine. "Yes, you could. But I would encourage you to stick around a few days. Sit on the beach. Let the waves lap at your toes. Maybe do a little snorkeling and let the South Pacific wash all the pompous off you. And then go back to the mainland a little *sunnier* of a human being."

"Go, Aunt Jenna!" Emma cheered from the sidelines.

The unsympathetic businessman wasn't having it. "I'll have your firm shut down."

Jenna opened her mouth right as her father's large hand clamped down on Barrington's shoulder. Orville Barrington might command a room, but he was just a small fish in Jim Burke's very deep ocean—and nobody threatened one of the Burke girls in their father's presence and got away with it.

"*Aloha*," Jim said. "What do you say we go to my place and I'll crack open a coconut for us to sip on."

The invitation didn't end with a question mark. Barrington

LINDY MILLER WITH TERENCE BRODY

dared a glance at Jim's muscular arms and withered. Clearly he preferred to dose out his intimidating persona, but wasn't equipped to be on the receiving end of the same.

"Oh, thank you," he replied, stammering just a tad, "but I should probably be going. It would appear our business here is concluded."

"Another time," Jim added for good measure. "Besides, I don't think Ms. Murray would take too kind to knowing her star designer was threatened on her own land. Bad for business, that sort of thing."

He removed his hand and winked at Jenna as Darren escorted the rattled man to their car. After shutting Barrington inside the rental, Darren turned back to Jenna. He lifted a finger and made to say something, but Jenna beat him to it by picking up the papers from the hood of Mike's car and tearing them in half. Whatever Darren might have said died unspoken on his tongue, and he shook his head and slid into the driver's seat.

The entire family watched as Darren put the car in reverse and escaped out of the driveway. Then, they all turned to stare at the house.

"What now, sis?" Sarah reached over and gave Jenna's hand a reassuring squeeze.

Jenna's heart fluttered—half excitement, half nerves—and she started toward the house. She wasn't sure what came next, not exactly, but whatever it was, it was waiting for her inside Aunt May's.

❧

She found Ben coming around a corner in the living room, carrying a vase with a large tropical flower arrangement. He looked at Jenna, and though she'd expected him to be wearing the same stiff poker face she'd seen him in before, the expression on his face was soft, almost eager. He looked so bashful Jenna almost forgot she'd been angry with him.

Almost.

"I don't know if you saw," she said, "but I just sent Darren and Barrington packing. And I tore up the contract."

Ben smirked, but kept his tone even. "Didn't mean to overhear, but I was watching the whole thing through the window."

"Eavesdropper," Jenna teased, letting her guard down a fraction.

"I like to think of it as hyper-observant," Ben shot back.

Shaking her head, Jenna allowed herself to take in the room around her. Though they'd been mostly finished before, the renovation was now as complete on the inside as it was on the outside. Ben had even staged the rooms with beautiful, hand carved furniture and a charming rustic beach chic décor. The empty rooms were now full—with warmth, with furnishings. With life. Her eyes stung, leaked.

Ben reached up and wiped a tear from her cheek. "This is it right here," he said, showing her the tear. "This is the look I wanted to see on your face."

Jenna smoothed away the dampness under her eyes and sniffled. More tears fell, and Ben pulled a clean rag from his pocket and dabbed them away, too.

His touch was gentle. "Liquid emotion. The best kind."

She managed a smile. How come no one had ever told her how heavy happiness could be? Still, the memory of who she had been, and what she had told herself, the day she'd lost her pitch and Darren had broken up with her over lunch hadn't changed entirely. The budding young architect who'd worked so hard to emulate her mentor was still inside. "You're not supposed to cry at work," she sniffed. "And since you're still working, I'm still considering this our project."

Ben shook his head and laughed. "But that's it exactly, isn't it? You told me you live for the first impression a job makes on a client. Well, that was my wish, too, for the first time you walked in here."

He was right. She had told him that. She'd told Ben that look was what made it all worthwhile—when a client walked into a finished job and wiped away a few tears of happiness. Those were the moments she lived for, the ones that made her do what she did.

"It's more beautiful than I could have ever imagined. Outside and in." Jenna looked up at Ben, at his blue eyes and dimples and stubborn but loveable face. "But I don't understand. Why did you do all this when you thought we would be tearing it all down?"

Ben put his arm around her shoulder and led her farther into the house. "I figured Aunt May paid for the job to be done right. I had to finish the house, even if the bulldozers were on their way. And, because I owe you an apology."

Jenna wanted to argue about the bulldozers but resisted the urge. Instead, she quirked an eyebrow and color bloomed in Ben's cheeks. He lifted a hand and ran his fingers through his dirty-blond hair, looking sheepish.

"The floors," he explained. "It wasn't my call to bring in the hardwood. I should have discussed it with you. We've been working together, but this is your house—your budget—and I should have been more respectful of that, instead of making assumptions on my own." He took her hand and pressed it between his, as he stared into her eyes. Sincere, genuine swirled inside the sunburst around his pupil. "I'm sorry. Truly."

Two little words, so small and yet, so important. Even the best of partners had disagreements, opportunities to apologize. The important part wasn't the argument, it was overcoming it and finding a way forward—together.

That, Jenna considered as she stared at the floor at her feet, *and the hardwood floors do look amazing.* Perhaps she could have been a little more open-minded, too—and a little less focused on her budget. After all, she didn't want to end up like Orville Barrington. The thought made her smile. She'd come close, hadn't she? Saving a few bucks on flooring over the undeniable beauty—and sustainability—of the real thing.

"Thank you," she said, accepting Ben's apology. "And you were right," she added. "The hardwood looks amazing."

Ben winked. "Told you."

"But how did you do all this? Forty-eight hours ago, you were packing up to go—and you're just a one man crew. This—" She took another look around. "This is a miracle."

"Small island, big miracles," Ben agreed. "Everyone here loved Aunt May. Loves you, too, and your dad and sister. So I called in all the favors I could, rounded up anyone willing to lend a hand, and we got her done. I wanted you to see her like this, *really* see her, even if it was just once."

"I do." Jenna did. She touched Ben's shoulder and then stepped away, moving through the rooms. All the spaces she'd loved so much as a girl flooded her heart with joy. If only May could see it now, see how beautiful her house looked and know how much love the island had put into it. How much love they had for her and her home.

Jenna paused in the living room, taking in the view of the ocean through a large window in the eastern facing wall—crystal blue sea, powder blue sky, and vibrant green palms.

"You even gave me my whale window," she said. *My* whale window. "You know, I never thought this about May's house until I walked in here today, but you made this a home I could see myself living in someday."

Ben shook his head. "We—*we*—made this a home."

Jenna's eyebrow lifted at the use of the plural pronoun and Ben laughed. "Even if I do have to have the furniture back in a few days."

"All rented?"

"All except one."

As if on cue, Jenna's father rounded the corner, carrying his finished, gleamingly polished kou wood coffee table. It was magnificent. The wood gleamed and the hibiscus and ivy carved on the legs seemed almost alive.

"Oh, Dad," Jenna gasped. "You finished it. It's gorgeous."

"Yes, it is," Jim agreed with a laugh. He set the table in the empty spot directly under the whale window and stepped back, beaming, and winked at Ben. "What do you think, Ben? Fits just like it was made to go there, doesn't it?"

"Perfect."

Jenna caught on. "So you were in on this little conspiracy, Dad?"

"Oh, from the very beginning," Ben confirmed. "He was one of the favors I called in."

"The *first* one," Jim Burke corrected. He gave Jenna a hug, held her for a moment, and then released her, nudging her just a teensy bit in Ben's direction as he turned to go. "I'm going to go make sure what's-his-name and the Big Kahuna developer are on their way to the airport."

The dried spots Jenna's tears had left on her skin cracked as she broke into laughter. She'd seen her father grieve, and she'd seen him sad and even angry, but there was nothing better than seeing him in his truest form—happy and full of life.

"So, what changed your mind out there?" Ben asked when they had the room to themselves again.

What had changed her mind? Jenna wasn't sure. There had been many things that had contributed to her change of heart, if she was willing to call it that, but one thing stuck out in particular.

"Something my Aunt May said to me about being with people who cherish me for who I am, not for what I can do for them. My whole life, I think I've been trying to be that other person. Someone I'm not, not really. Trying to earn their love instead of just opening my arms to the people who already love me."

Ben moved in closer. Jenna felt heat against her back where his arm encircled her. "And who already loves you?" he asked.

Jenna looked up into his bright, Hawaiian sky blue eyes and studied the little flecks of gold circling his pupils. "My Aunt May was one, and my dad and sister. I know my family cares for me like that."

"Anyone else?"

Jenna lifted her arms and clasped her hands around Ben's neck, drawing him toward her. "Ben, even though I gave up on you, you didn't give up on this old house." She pulled him closer. "Or on me."

Ben lowered his head and their foreheads touched. His lips brushed against hers. "Never."

Jenna thought about teasing him. She thought about

reminding him of all the ups and downs, the arguments, the bruised egos and busted thumbs. But she didn't. Jenna took one more look inside the paradise of Ben's eyes and then pressed her lips against his.

Chapter Twenty-Five

Three Months Later

The dining room that had once belonged to Aunt May was full of the mouthwatering aromas of coconut and lemon, and the wide open rooms were full of light, love, and family. Jenna sat on the newly built back porch, watching the bright blue sky deepen into brilliant hues of crimson and amber as the sun set over the horizon. The view was much the same as it had been when she'd sat on this porch with May as a girl, but the feeling was different now. Now, Jenna was home.

"I can't believe you ever thought of tearing this place down," Ben teased as he joined her on the porch. He sat in the chair beside her and reached down to lovingly pat the wooden plank at his feet. "Poor old gal really dodged a bullet on that one."

This had become a familiar jest over the past couple of months, usually at particularly beautiful moments—sunrises, sunsets, and midnight trips out to stare at the starry sky over the water on the horizon. Teasing Jenna must have been a line item in May's renovation budget that wasn't quite spent.

"I already told you, I never *wanted* to tear the house down," Jenna retorted playfully. "Just took me a while to come around to keeping her is all. Sort of like you."

Ben feigned offense. "Touche."

Sarah and Emma emerged through the back door, Jim hot on their heels. Both women were carrying trays heaped with finger foods and traditional Hawaiian desserts—crab cakes and sweet 'n' sour meatballs, and pineapple upside down cake, haupia cupcakes, and fruit kabobs.

"Hope you guys are hungry!" Sarah set the trays on the small outdoor dining table, swatting away her father's hand before it could snatch a crab cake. Jim grumbled and retreated back inside, no doubt to root amongst the cooking scraps in the kitchen. "Dad's on the prowl. Better get it while it's hot."

Jenna and Ben both reached forward. Ben quickly dispatched a crab cake while Jenna opted for one of the fragrant haupia cupcakes. She unwrapped the pastry and took a healthy bite of the creamy coconut treat. Still warm from the oven, the cupcake filled her mouth with flavors she hadn't experienced since she was a girl. She moaned her appreciation to the chef, and stuffed the rest of the cake in her mouth, then licked a stray dollop of frosting from her finger and gave her sister a thumbs up.

"Actually," Sara returned, drawing the word out. She crinkled her nose coyly at her daughter. "Emma made the haupia. Not sure where it comes from, but it would appear my girl's got a knack for baking."

"Oh my—" Jenna managed around a mouthful of creamy cupcake.

"—goodness," Ben finished, swallowing down the last of his cupcake.

Emma grinned. "I learned from the best chef I know. My mom."

The look on her niece's face was even sweeter than her cupcake, and Jenna felt the impact in her chest. Somewhere in all this, Sarah and Emma had found their way back to one another as mom and daughter, and Jenna was so grateful. Even Ethan had been spending more time with the family—though his trusty handheld video game console was never far behind. Baby steps.

A mischievous thought tickled against Jenna's tongue and she sneaked a peek at Ben before catching Sarah's attention. "By the way, I drove by Grandma's Coffee House today, and the *For Sale* sign has been taken down."

Sarah's face fell. "Really? Oh well. I hope somebody makes good use of the property."

"Me, too." Jenna signaled to Ben. He reached behind a large potted ivy—the same one Grace had sent to May's funeral—and pulled something hidden behind it into view. The *For Sale* sign.

"Wait—what?" Sarah's crestfallen face had taken on a slightly deer-in-headlights sort of appearance: eyes wide, mouth agape.

Jenna stood, took the sign from Ben, and handed it to her sister. "You better get busy, sis. You're the new owner."

The deer on Jenna's new back porch blinked. "How?"

"I sold my LA condo, and you won't *believe* how much I got for nine-hundred square feet," Jenna explained honestly. Truthfully, it was a little embarrassing how much money she'd squandered on an apartment the size of a shoebox. She'd completed the transaction on her own, too. Apparently she'd learned just enough about real estate during her time with Darren to be dangerous—and capable. Imagine that.

"Enough to buy a bakery?"

"*O 'oe ke hele.*" Jenna smiled at her sister. She had her dream, and now, Sarah had hers.

Once she'd blinked herself back to reality, Sarah threw her arms around Jenna's neck. She squeezed. Danced in place. Squeezed harder. "Oh, Jenna ... *Mahalo, Mahalo!*" Still bounding with excitement, Sarah released Jenna and then constricted herself around Ben before gathering her family in her arms.

Jim appeared on the porch, armed with a celebratory round of piña coladas and mai-tais. He set the beverage tray beside the pastry trays on the table, quickly swallowed down a crabcake, and opened his arms to his oldest daughter. "Sarah's Bakery is going to be fantastic!"

Sarah punched a playful fist into her father's meaty bicep. "Wait, you knew?"

"Papa knows everything," he teased.

"Not everything!" A sharp female voice rang out from inside the house, followed by short-cropped blonde hair. Patti Murray poked her head through the doors of the patio. Like Jenna, she'd traded in her slick city business wardrobe for island casual, and she looked great. "Figured if Jenna's going to be heading up our new Hawaiian branch of Avery Architects, I'd better take an official business trip down to the islands to see it for myself."

Jenna gaped. She'd known Patti had planned a trip to the islands, but had never expected her to show up unannounced—until she saw the woman plant a kiss on her father's cheek.

"Your orange slices, my love," Patti said, then slipped a sliver of the fruit onto the rim of one of the mai-tais.

Jim put his arm around her and pulled her in, kissing her quickly on the lips. "What would I do without you?"

Jenna and Sarah exchanged a look of utter bewilderment. When had *this* happened?

Patti dismissed the look of shock on Jenna's face and took a seat at the table beside her. "I'm so glad you convinced me that a second branch was such a good idea," she said. Her face broke into a kind of grin Jenna had never seen the woman wear. It changed her completely, transforming the buttoned-up businesswoman into an island free spirit. "Well, you *and* your father."

A dozen questions queued in Jenna's mind, but she took one look at the smile on her dad's and Patti's faces, and let them go. Who cared about the details when such happiness was evident?

"Now you just have to make it permanent like I did," she said.

"I never thought I'd even consider leaving the city," Patti admitted. Then she looked at Jim. "But I just may. Who knew an RV-living, mullet-headed surfer would check all my boxes?"

Jenna snuggled herself inside Ben's arms. "Island boys tend to do that."

The rest of Jenna's family gathered around the table and quiet fell over the group as they all lost themselves in the beauty of a Hawaiian sunset. In the distance, right where the strawberry bushes had begun to bloom at the edge of the property line against the dense tropical jungle, Jenna could almost see the figure of an old woman in a white muumuu with a bright red lei around her neck.

The woman smiled and raised a hand. *Aloha*, May called, her voice as rich and vibrant in Jenna's memory as it had been in life.

Aloha, Aunt May. Jenna blinked back a tear and laid her head against Ben's shoulder.

He brushed a light kiss on her cheek. "Welcome home, Jenna."

Jenna smiled, but her heart was too full of love and gratitude to reply as she looked out across her grass, her ocean … her Aloha.

HAUPIA CAKE

Ingredients

For the Cake:

- 1 box white cake mix
- 1 cup coconut milk, separated
- 2/3 cup water
- 2 egg whites
- 1 tablespoon unflavored gelatin
- 2 cups heavy cream
- 6 tablespoon granulated sugar
- 1 teaspoon lemon extract
- 1-2 cups shredded coconut (to sprinkle over cake)

For the Haupia Filling:

- 1 cup granulated sugar
- ½ teaspoon salt
- 6 tablespoon cornstarch
- 1 cup water
- 4 cups coconut milk, not separated
- 2 teaspoons vanilla

Method

1. Preheat oven according to directions on cake mix box.
2. Prepare two 8 or 9-inch round cake pans.
3. Prepare cake mix according to package directions, using 2/3 cup of the coconut milk, water, and egg whites.
4. Bake cake according to package directions. When cooled, cut each cake horizontally into two layers, making sure they are flat. Set aside.

5. Soften gelatin in remaining 1/3 cup of coconut milk. Dissolve over hot water, and cool completely.
6. For the frosting: In a large mixing bowl, whip the heavy cream. Fold in the gelatin mixture, sugar, and lemon extract. Chill frosting until it is spreadable.
7. For the filling: In a small bowl, mix together sugar, salt, cornstarch, and water. Set aside.
8. In a saucepan, heat the coconut milk. When hot, add sugar mixture. Cook, stirring constantly, until thickened.
9. Remove vanilla and cool. Chill until spreadable.
10. To assemble: Spread the Haupia filling between each cake layer, about ½" thick. Stack and refrigerate until set. Frost the entire cake with whipped cream mixture. Sprinkle coconut over the cake's top and sides. Keep refrigerated until ready to serve. Enjoy!

HAWAIIAN STRAWBERRY PIE

Ingredients

- 1 premade graham cracker pie crust
- 2 cups sliced fresh strawberries*
- 3 ounces strawberry gelatin
- 3.5 ounces vanilla pudding (not instant)
- 8 ounces crushed pineapple (drain and reserve juice)
- 1 teaspoon coconut extract
- 1 cup whipped cream
- 2 tablespoons flaked coconut, sweetened
- 1 cup water

2 cups frozen, unsweetened, drained strawberries may be substituted

Method

1. Place strawberries in frozen pie crust.
2. In a medium saucepan, combine the dry gelatin and pudding mix.
3. Add enough water to make the pineapple juice reach 1 ½ cups liquid. Add to pudding mixture.
4. Cook pudding mixture over medium heat, stirring constantly, until mixture thickens and comes to a gentle boil.
5. Remove pudding mixture from head and pour over strawberries. Refrigerate 2 hours.
6. In a small bowl, combine the drained pineapple, coconut extract, and whipped cream. Mix gently to combine. Keep cool.

7. To assemble: When pie is completely cool, spread the pineapple mixture over the set strawberry filling and sprinkle coconut flakes over the top, as desired.

8. Refrigerate until set, about 10 minutes—and enjoy!

TOASTED COCONUT CREAM PUDDING

Ingredients

- 14 ounces shredded coconut, sweetened
- 2 packages (3.4 ounces) coconut pudding
- 2 cups milk
- 14 ounces sweetened condensed milk*
- 1 ½ cups heavy whipping cream
- 1/3 cup confectioners' sugar
- 2 teaspoons vanilla extract
- 1 box vanilla wafers

for extra coconut flavor, you may also substitute with cream of coconut

Method

1. Preheat oven to 425 degrees.
2. Spread coconut in an even layer on a parchment paper lined cookie sheet.
3. Bake coconut for 6 minutes, turning between.
4. In a large mixing bowl, whisk together powdered pudding mix and condensed milk. Let sit for 3 minutes.
5. In a separate large bowl (or stand mixer on low speed), beat whipping cream, powdered sugar, and vanilla extract until peaks form.
6. Fold whipped cream into pudding mix until smooth.
7. To assemble: In a large bowl (or smaller individual jars), layer 1/3 of vanilla wafers across bottom, then 1/3 toasted coconut, then 1/3 pudding. Repeat with two more layers, ending with toasted coconut as garnish—and enjoy!

Acknowledgements

To Italia Gandolfo and Liana Gardner, for collectively being my Patti Murray—except with fewer tissues and lots more laughs and cat gifs. I appreciate and love you both dearly.

To Holly Atkinson and Najla Qamber, for your careful editing and expert vision. It takes a village to bring a story to life, and I am grateful to have such incredible women in my tribe.

To Ildiko McCabe, for single-handedly helping me build my writing playlist as I wrote this book—and for always bringing much needed sunshine to the cold days of Alaska.

To Lindsey Neumann, for being my favorite neighbor—and my open invite to visit the islands!

To Wake, my favorite travel companion. I'm so lucky to be your mom. Even on red-eye flights.

And, of course, to Finn, for hours spent curled beneath my feet, listening to me type.

About The Authors

 Lindy Miller is an award-wining author of feel-good love stories full of sweet moments and happy endings. She believes the best time to fall in love is during the holidays, preferably over a cup of warm tea or a delicious vegan pastry - two things she can't get enough of.

A free spirit, Lindy loves to travel and believes there's nothing that can't be cured with salt, seawater, and sunshine. She is married to her childhood sweetheart and bakes as often as she can for her husband, son, and pets - especially her golden retriever, Finn, who has a tendency to show up in her stories (and her social media!).

Lindy is represented by Gandolfo Helin & Fountain Literary Management and supported by Smith Publicity.

Member Romantic Novelist Association (RNA) and Romance Writers of America (RWA).

www.LindyMillerRomance

Terence Brody is an active captain on the FDNY, assigned to Ladder 10 in lower Manhattan.

Two of his feature scripts, RESCUING MADISON (Ethan Peck, C. Thomas Howell, Alona Tal) and A LESSON IN ROMANCE (Kristy Swanson, Scott Grimes, directed by Ron Oliver) aired on the Hallmark Channel.

His script, RENOVATE MY HEART, produced by Brian Bird of *When Calls The Heart* and Branscombe Richmond, is in pre-production, and the novel co-written with author Lindy Miller releases Summer 2021. Brody also wrote the screenplay for Miller's novel *Sleigh Bells on Bread Loaf Mountain* (2021) and *The Christmas Spirit* by Alexandrea Weis (Nov 2020).

Brody resides in Long Island, NY with his wife and two children.

www.imdb.com/name/nm3255750/